THE SEA ISLE SUMMER RENTAL

CLAUDIA VANCE

CHAPTER ONE

Meredith had told them it was nice, which was true—just not the whole truth.

What she hadn't mentioned was the upgrade. The original rental had fallen through in April. Meredith had found this one instead: oceanfront on 59th Street, a newer beach house with cream vinyl siding, three stacked decks facing the water, a rooftop terrace with an outdoor kitchen and built-in bar, a private pool tucked along the side of the house with a hot tub beside it, another hot tub on the rooftop, a ground-floor game room with a pool table and foosball. She'd paid the difference herself without a word to anyone. A place like this in Sea Isle City in June didn't come cheap.

Meredith stood at the railing of the rooftop terrace and looked straight out at the ocean. From up here you could see the whole stretch of it—the white break of the waves, the long flat line of the horizon, the beach still packed with umbrellas and chairs all the way to the water's edge. The air was warm and salt-heavy, settling on your skin within a minute of being outside.

She'd told her husband, Tom, obviously, and he'd said, "Whatever you think"—which was enough. She had not told the other women. Partly because it wasn't relevant, and partly because Meredith had always preferred to let things arrive before she explained them.

She could already tell it had worked.

"Mom." Sophie appeared in the doorway behind her, phone pressed to her collarbone, her signal that she was mid-conversation and didn't want to be interrupted. "Can I claim the bedroom with the double windows? The one facing the street side?"

"We're doing rooms when everyone gets here."

"I just want to call it."

"That's not how this works."

She disappeared back inside, and Meredith could hear her footsteps on the stairs and then Trevor's voice carrying faintly from the phone as Sophie found a corner to finish her conversation. Trevor was a good kid. Safe, predictable. Meredith wasn't worried about Trevor.

Meredith was more worried about Sophie spending the entire summer with one foot back home.

She turned away from the ocean, taking in the street side. Below, 59th Street was filling up—people hauling wagons of beach gear, a couple of bikes cruising past, kids in swim trunks cutting through the alley between houses with a boogie board tucked under each arm. Sea Isle in June had its own energy— not yet the full crush of July, but enough that you could feel the season ahead of you. A woman in a wide sun hat was power-walking with a coffee in one hand and a leash wrapped around the other, connected to a golden retriever doing its best to move in the same direction. From somewhere two houses over came the smell of someone firing up a grill.

All summer, Meredith thought. Let's see what we do with all summer.

They'd been talking about it for years—a whole summer at the shore, all of them together, the way they used to do long weekends in their twenties before mortgages and marriages and kids made everything harder to schedule. Back when they were just five girls who'd met freshman year at Rowan and didn't know yet how much they'd need each other.

She went downstairs to finish unpacking and got distracted by the living area, which made her pause at the threshold. Floor-to-ceiling windows ran the length of the ocean side, and beyond them was the beach and then nothing but water—wide and blue and close enough that you could track the individual waves. The kitchen flowed into it without a seam, the kind of open-concept layout that real estate listings called seamless and that actually was, for once. Quartz countertops, a six-burner gas range, a farmhouse sink deep enough to wash a baking sheet standing upright. She opened the cabinets one by one out of professional habit—real estate had made her incapable of entering a kitchen without doing inventory—and found them fully stocked. Not the usual mismatched rental hodgepodge but actual sets: Crate and Barrel dishes, wine glasses that weren't plastic. The hall closet, checked on a hunch, held White Company linens. She closed the last door and exhaled.

She pulled out her phone and texted Tom a photo of the kitchen.

He wrote back thirty seconds later: *You're never coming home, are you?*

She smiled and put her phone away.

* * *

The others arrived in waves over the next hour—cars double-parked, bags hauled up the front steps, teenagers scattering in four directions before the engines were even off. By the time the last bag was through the front door, the house was loud.

Carrie was in the kitchen, reorganizing the cabinet she'd already reorganized once, moving the glasses Meredith had put away to a lower shelf she found more logical. Her daughters were gone. Brittany was upstairs, Ava somewhere with her

3

camera. Lori was on the middle deck with a tray of iced coffees from Shorebreak, calling out to Ethan to grab the cooler from the car. He ignored her. Jen had taken a corner of the living room to drop her things and was at the windows, staring at the ocean like she was trying to decide if it was real. Olivia's twins had located the Bluetooth speaker and were arguing over whose phone to connect; Olivia herself stood at the bottom of the staircase with a duffel bag over each shoulder, reading a text, then reading it again.

"Rooms," Meredith said from the kitchen doorway. "We need to do rooms before anyone unpacks anywhere."

"I already called the one with the double windows," Sophie said from somewhere upstairs.

Meredith leaned against the doorframe. "Calling it doesn't count."

"I know. I'm just saying."

Lori came in from the deck, coffee tray still in hand. "This house, Meredith. I need you to know that I almost cried pulling up."

"You did not almost cry," Carrie said, eyes on the cabinet.

"I teared up a little. The rooftop alone—"

"Nobody is going to the rooftop until we do rooms," Meredith said.

Jen raised her hand. "I'd like to formally request a single."

"There are six bedrooms." Meredith shrugged. "We'll make it work."

That settled things enough to get everyone moving. The next twenty minutes were a blur—doors opening and closing, someone asking where the extra towels were, footsteps in every direction.

Jen stood in the middle of the living room, suitcase still at her feet, watching it all unfold. "This is why I have a cat," she said to no one.

Sophie claimed the upstairs corner room, the one with the double windows, before anyone could argue. Brittany tossed her bag on the other bed—college sophomore and high school senior, close enough in age to coexist. Sophie was on the phone with Trevor before Brittany had even unzipped her suitcase. Lily and Ava ended up together in the room with the twin beds —Lily's idea, which Ava accepted with a shrug, though Meredith noticed Ava immediately began shifting the furniture while Lily narrated the whole operation from her side of the room. Max took the converted sunroom off the back of the main floor, smallest room in the house, its own side entrance. Ethan took the second bed. Meredith suspected Max had chosen the room in about four seconds flat, and Ethan had followed for exactly the same reason—away from the adults.

Olivia got her own room. Nobody questioned it.

Jen looked at Meredith. "So much for my single."

"You'll survive," Meredith said, dropping her bag onto the bed by the window.

Carrie and Lori took the room across the hall. Meredith could hear them negotiating closet space.

Once the bags were mostly where they needed to be, Meredith looked around. "Rooftop."

Nobody needed to be asked twice.

The outdoor staircase opened onto the terrace, and the group spread out across it slowly, the space bigger than they'd expected—each person finding the edge or the railing or a spot at the built-in bar, taking it in. The outdoor kitchen ran along the front wall: a full grill, counters, a mini fridge built into the base. A hot tub sat in the corner, jets off, cover still on. Teak lounge chairs lined the perimeter. And in every direction— ocean to the east, bay glinting to the west, the narrow stretch of the island in between—it was all open sky.

Brittany had her phone up, slowly panning. Lily stood at the railing, looking down at the beach. Lori leaned against the bar, speechless.

"The bar has a sink," Jen said, peering behind it. "And a blender."

"It has a blender," Meredith said.

"I'm just confirming." Jen opened the mini fridge. "Empty, but cold. Someone's going to need to make a store run."

"Tomorrow."

"Tonight," Jen said. "I brought rosé." She held it up. "First order of business is figuring out who has the best blender drink recipe."

"That is not the first order of business," Meredith said.

"It's in the top three," Carrie said.

They stayed up there longer than they meant to. Eventually people drifted back downstairs to finish unpacking, the rooftop releasing them one at a time.

Meredith stopped in Carrie and Lori's doorway on her way past with an armful of extra towels. Lori had wandered back to the deck, but Carrie was unpacking in neat stacks—shirts by color, shorts folded in even halves, toiletry bag hung on the back of the bathroom door.

"You okay?" Meredith asked.

Carrie didn't stop folding. "I'm really good." She pressed a shirt flat against the top of the dresser. "I brought four bottles of wine, two of which are from the Whole Foods sale section because I am trying to be financially responsible." She looked up. "And one extremely unnecessary cheese board from the specialty counter because I am also trying to live my life." She set the shirt in the drawer. "So, I'm somewhere in the middle."

Meredith leaned against the doorframe. "The cheese board sounds right to me."

Carrie laughed—a real one. "Good. Because I already opened it."

Meredith left her to it.

She was halfway down the hall when she heard the back gate open, then Brittany's voice, then Ava's, then Lily's—a chain reaction of doors and footsteps that ended with most of the women standing on the side path looking at a twelve-by-twenty-four rectangle of blue water with a sun shelf on one end and two built-in loungers submerged on the other. The pool sat in a private courtyard, tucked between the house and a low dune ridge thick with sea grass. You couldn't see the ocean from here, but you could hear it. The steady roll of waves just beyond the dunes. The hot tub was nestled in the corner, half-hidden by ornamental grasses, and someone had strung market lights along the fence line.

"I want to be clear," Brittany said, "that I am getting in this pool before the end of the day."

"It's five o'clock," Lori said.

"Correct." Brittany was already eyeing the sun shelf.

Olivia crouched down and put her hand in. "It's warm."

"The sun shelf," Carrie said, pointing. "You can sit in there with a drink."

"That's where I'll be," Lori said.

At the pool's edge, Lily sat with her feet in. "Tonight?" she said, hopeful.

Meredith glanced at the pool, then at the six teens now assembled around it, all of them eyeing the water. "Tomorrow," she said. "Tonight we eat."

A unified groan. She ignored it.

She had almost reached the kitchen when she heard it—not a cautious feet-first entry but a full, committed, cannonball-grade launch. She turned around.

Max surfaced fully clothed, still in his shorts and T-shirt. He pushed his hair out of his face, looking around at the faces staring back.

"Had to be done," he said.

Lily put her face in her hands. Olivia closed her eyes briefly. Ethan, who had not smiled once since he arrived, laughed.

Lori, standing by the gate, went very still. Meredith caught her eye. Neither of them said anything.

"You're an idiot," Lily said.

"You're just mad you didn't do it first," Max said, floating on his back now, sneakers still on.

Meredith pointed at him. "Shoes by the door."

* * *

Over the next hour, everyone scattered.

Olivia spent most of that hour on the upper deck, book open in her lap but untouched. Her phone was in her hand instead, and Meredith watched through the sliding door as she typed something, deleted it, typed again. Not her husband—her face was wrong for Dan. At one point her phone rang. She looked at the screen, set it face-down, and did not answer.

By six o'clock the kids had sorted themselves out—on their own, as expected. Lily and Sophie had taken over the top deck, and when Meredith passed by she caught a fragment: Sophie asking what it was like being a twin, Lily saying, "Like having a shadow that talks back." Both of them laughing.

Ava had set herself up on the far corner of the lower deck with her camera and a glass of lemonade, photographing everything except the obvious. Not the waves or the wide open sky, but the small things. The shadow the railing threw across the deck boards. A seagull perched on a neighboring rooftop. The screen door's mesh catching the early evening light.

Meredith had stopped at the Acme on the way in and picked up the basics—deli turkey, ham, roast beef, three kinds of cheese, two loaves of bread, tomatoes, lettuce, mustard, mayo, a jar of pickles, and two bags of chips. She laid it all out on the counter and said dinner was ready.

"This is genius," Brittany said, building hers.

"This is a sandwich," Lori said.

"First night is always sandwiches," Meredith said. "I don't make the rules."

"You absolutely make the rules," Jen said, slicing tomatoes.

Carrie came in from the living room and surveyed the counter. "Did you get pickles?"

Meredith slid the jar toward her. "Whole jar."

"Then I'm good." She reached past Brittany for the rye.

They ate in the kitchen and on the sectional and out on the middle deck, plates balanced on laps, nobody sitting anywhere in particular.

After, Jen said she'd spotted a sign for ice cream earlier—was someone going to walk with her, or was she doing this alone?

Everyone went.

The house was two blocks from the southern end of the promenade—close enough that you could hear it before you reached it, the distant thrum of a cover band up near JFK, the hum of bikes going past. They walked up in a loose cluster, the kids pulling ahead, the women falling into the easy pace that came from years of knowing each other. The promenade was lit and busy, Sea Isle on a summer evening—families walking, teenagers moving in groups, the ocean right there on one side and a long row of houses on the other.

Yum Yums was just off the promenade on JFK. There was a line out the door; two of the women suggested turning back, but nobody actually did. Jen got a waffle cone and ate it while walking and declared it one of the better decisions she'd made recently. Lily and Sophie split a sundae. Ava got a single scoop of something dark chocolate and photographed it before eating it.

"You know you can just eat it," Brittany said.

"You know you can just not comment," Ava said, not looking up.

Brittany turned to Meredith. "I like her."

On the way back they took the promenade instead of the street. The air had gone cooler, the ocean shifted from blue to something darker. Nobody said much.

They were almost back to the house when Lily stopped and

pointed west. The sky over the mainland had gone apricot and deep rose. "Okay," she said. "It's actually happening."

Someone said rooftop. That was enough—everyone moving, up the front steps, through the house, up the outdoor stairs, drinks retrieved along the way.

The western sky was on fire now—pinks bleeding into orange, the last bright band of gold along the horizon. Behind them the ocean side still held that flat blue before dark. The street below had gone quiet, beach crowd long since retreated, and the sound of the water carried in from the east. From a few streets over came the faint pulse of a restaurant patio. A sprinkler somewhere nearby. A neighbor's wind chime making an effort.

Five women on a deck in Sea Isle City in June. Meredith took a sip of her wine and didn't try to name it.

"We should toast," Lily said, her glass of iced tea held up.

Brittany raised an eyebrow. "You want to do a toast?"

"Okay, someone should do a toast," Lily amended.

Everyone looked at Meredith, because everyone always looked at Meredith, and she felt the familiar pull of being expected to find the right words.

She raised her glass. "To Sea Isle."

It landed easily, and the women raised their glasses—Carrie from her chair, Olivia at the railing, Lori at the far end, Jen in the middle—and the kids joined in from the steps, ragged and good-natured. To Sea Isle.

The sky deepened another shade.

Meredith looked out over the street and thought about Tom, probably home right now with cereal beside his laptop, modeling whatever early retirement scenario he was testing this week. Then Sophie, leaving in the fall, and how she was both ready and not, and how she had the whole summer to figure out what came after.

The colors peaked and then faded. No one moved to go inside yet. The first few stars showed up over the water.

To Sea Isle, Meredith thought, watching the sky go dark.

CHAPTER TWO

The checklist was sunscreen, towels, cooler, chairs, speaker—
and eleven people who had agreed to leave at nine and were
now treating that as a suggestion.

By the front door, beach bag over one shoulder, Meredith
watched the house fail to mobilize. Carrie was looking for the
beach tags. Sophie and Brittany had already left. Somewhere
upstairs, Ethan had not responded to the last three times Lori
had called his name.

"Beach tags," Meredith said. "Who has them?"

From behind the kitchen island, Carrie held up a zippered
pouch. "Got them."

"Ethan. We're leaving." Lori was at the top of the
stairs now.

"I heard you." His voice came through the door, flat and
unmoving.

She stood there a moment longer, hand on the railing.
Then she came down without him.

The walk to the beach should have been simple. It wasn't.
Someone went back for the speaker. Then someone went back
for the speaker charger. Then Olivia pointed out that Carrie
had been holding the speaker the entire time.

"I thought this was the sunscreen," Carrie said, looking at it.

"The sunscreen is in the bag," Meredith said.

"Then what have I been putting on my arms?" Lori asked.

Carrie looked at Lori's arms. Lori looked at her own.

The beach at 59th was busy—umbrellas and pop-up tents staked out in clusters, chairs angled toward the water, the first round of sand castles underway near the break. Two lifeguards sat high in the stand, scanning the surf. The waves were rolling in clean sets, not big, the kind that were perfect for just standing in the break and letting it push you sideways. The air smelled like salt and sunscreen, and somewhere nearby a radio hummed with a song none of them recognized.

Sophie and Brittany had already claimed a spot about twenty feet back from the water, towels spread, sunglasses on, looking like they'd been there for hours. Setting up camp took twelve minutes and involved a negotiation about umbrella placement that nobody won.

By the time they had chairs arranged and the cooler positioned where everyone could reach it, the teenagers had scattered toward the water and were in—all except Ethan, who hadn't moved past the wet sand. Arms crossed, facing the horizon.

The women took the chairs. For a few minutes nobody said anything—just the ocean, the distant calls of kids down the beach, a lifeguard whistle somewhere.

"This is the thing," Jen said, face tilted toward the sun. "Right here. This is the thing."

Lori reclined and exhaled like she'd been waiting eight months for this chair. "What are we doing for lunch?"

"It's nine-thirty." Meredith didn't look up from her book.

"I'm thinking ahead."

"Wawa," Carrie said. "Hoagies."

"Done." Lori pointed at her.

They talked about nothing in particular after that—the

drive down, the weather forecast, whether anyone had remembered to bring cards for the evenings, whether the hot tub on the roof actually worked or was just for show. Carrie had already looked it up: it worked, but they'd need to wait twenty minutes for it to heat. Lori said she could wait. The conversation looped back on itself, easy with the quiet.

Dripping, towel wrapped around her shoulders, Sophie came up from the water. Sand clung to her calves. She'd walked past The Crabby Catch during the ice cream run last night and asked if they were hiring. Interview tomorrow at ten.

"That was fast," Meredith said.

"I saw the sign in the window." Sophie grinned. "Figured why not."

"You're going to be insufferable by August," Brittany said.

Sophie shoved her, and they headed back toward the surf, both of them laughing.

Lori's eyes found Ethan, still at the waterline. "He's applied to six places. Nothing back yet. Not even a no."

Down the beach, Sophie and Brittany were walking past the lifeguard stand. One of the guards—tan, dark hair, college-aged—glanced down at them. Brittany looked straight ahead, very deliberately not looking. Sophie didn't bother pretending.

"He looked," Sophie said, once they were past.

"I know." Brittany still didn't turn around. "I have peripheral vision."

"You should go talk to him."

"I'm not going to talk to him. He's working."

"He's sitting in a chair."

"He's watching for drowning people, Sophie."

"Nobody's drowning."

They kept walking toward the jetty, the sand hot under their feet. Sophie glanced back once. He was scanning the water again, left to right, but then he stopped. Looked right at her. She held it—a second, maybe two—and walked directly into a sandcastle.

"No," Sophie said, stumbling. A kid started wailing. The mom looked up from her phone.

"Keep walking," Brittany said, grabbing her arm. "Just keep walking."

"I destroyed it. I destroyed his whole castle."

"He'll rebuild. Walk."

They didn't stop until they were out of sight. Sophie looked back.

"He definitely saw that," Sophie said.

"Like, definitely."

"Stop."

"Peripheral vision," Brittany said, and Sophie bumped her so hard she almost fell.

* * *

Around eleven, Max and Lily volunteered for the Wawa run. Carrie handed over her card, and they headed back toward the house, their voices fading as they crossed the dune.

At the shoreline, Jen stood just inside the break, the water barely to her ankles. She'd said she needed to cool off and walked down ten minutes ago, and she was still there. Not watching the water, not looking at her phone. Just the tide around her feet and her arms crossed over her chest.

Lori had her eyes closed, might have been asleep. Olivia had her book open but hadn't turned a page in fifteen minutes.

The hoagies arrived. So did Jen, finally back from the water, dropping into her chair without a word.

"So." Carrie unwrapped hers and looked around at the group. "How is everyone? Actually."

A seagull landed on the cooler. Nobody moved fast enough. It grabbed a chip bag and was gone before Jen could get a hand up, wings beating hard as it lifted off toward the dunes.

"That's mine," Jen said.

"Was." Carrie was already laughing.

A second seagull landed. Then a third. Jen lunged at them with her book and they scattered, screaming, only to circle back and land three feet away.

"They're organizing," Lori said.

"They're not organizing." Jen tossed a chip toward the dunes to lure them away.

Two more seagulls landed.

"You just made it worse," Carrie said, wiping her eyes.

"I panicked."

When the laughter faded, nobody jumped in right away.

"Tom's retiring," Meredith said finally, because someone had to go first. "Or thinking about it. He's been running numbers for six months."

"That's good, right?" Lori asked.

"It's fine. It's just—" She stopped. "He'll be home. All the time."

"Ah," Jen said.

"I love him. I'm just not sure I want to see him that much."

None of them flinched. They'd known each other long enough that the ugly truths didn't need softening.

"Richard used to work from home on Fridays." Carrie half-smiled. "I'd hide in the laundry room."

"That's not the same," Olivia said.

"Yeah." Carrie picked at her chips, eyes somewhere else. "It's worse now. The house is too quiet."

The waves rolled in. Rolled out.

"Six months," Carrie said. "And I still expect to hear his car in the driveway."

"It gets easier." Lori reached over and squeezed her arm.

"Does it?"

"Easier isn't the right word." Lori thought about it. "You just stop waiting."

Carrie nodded, though she didn't look convinced.

Meredith turned to Olivia, who had been watching Max and Lily in the water—Max trying to catch a wave, Lily floating nearby on her back. "Dan coming down this weekend?"

No answer right away. Her eyes were on the water, or maybe on nothing at all.

"Dan had an affair," she said.

Nobody moved.

"What?" Carrie's voice came out strange.

"Emotional. Not physical. At least that's what he says." Olivia pulled at a thread on her beach towel, not looking at any of them. "A woman at work. They texted. All the time. For months."

"When did you find out?" Meredith asked.

"February. He left his phone on the counter and I saw her name." She lifted one shoulder, let it drop. "I wasn't looking. I just saw it."

No one said anything.

"We're trying. Counseling, date nights, all of it. He says it's over." She finally looked up. "I don't know if I believe him. I don't know if it matters."

"It matters," Jen said.

"Does it? He didn't sleep with her. He just—" She searched for the words. "He talked to her. About things he should have been talking to me about. And now I'm supposed to forgive that because it wasn't physical."

Carrie shook her head slowly. Lori put a hand on Olivia's shoulder.

"The kids don't know," Olivia said. "They know something's wrong. They're not stupid. But they don't know what."

"I'm sorry," Meredith said. "I didn't know."

"I didn't tell anyone." Olivia took a long sip of iced tea, her hand steady. "It's easier to pretend it's fine."

"It's not fine," Carrie said.

"No. It's not."

Carrie turned to Lori, shifting the weight. "And you? Anyone new?"

"No." Lori shook her head. "I'm not ready. I don't know if I'll ever be ready."

"You'll be ready," Jen said.

"Maybe." She didn't sound convinced. "It's been three years, and I still flinch when someone asks me out for coffee."

"Give it time," Olivia said.

"What about Ethan?" Meredith asked. "How's he doing with everything?"

Lori glanced toward the water. Ethan was sitting on the sand now, apart from the others. "Ethan doesn't think anything. Ethan doesn't talk."

"He's seventeen," Carrie said.

"He was talking fine until Kevin announced the engagement."

She hadn't meant to say it like that—hard, bitter. She took a breath.

"His dad's getting married again. To someone who's basically Sophie's age."

"She's not that young," Meredith said.

"She's thirty-two."

"Okay, she's young."

"And Ethan has to be in the wedding. Kevin wants him to be a groomsman." Lori exhaled. "He hasn't said yes. He hasn't said anything. He just—stopped."

Jen had been quiet through all of this, looking out at the water rather than at any of them.

Carrie nudged her. "Any news from the dating apps?"

"I deleted them."

"Again?" Carrie said.

"Permanently." Jen took a bite of her hoagie. "I've decided I'm done looking."

"You're forty-five," Lori said.

"And?"

"I'm just saying. There's time."

"I know there's time. That's not the point." She wiped her

hands on a napkin, slow and deliberate. "I spent twenty years waiting for the right person. Maybe they don't exist. Maybe I'm fine on my own."

"You're not fine," Olivia said. "You're writing a book about it."

Jen laughed, caught off guard. "That's different."

"Is it?"

"The book isn't about me."

"Sure." Olivia was grinning now.

A chip flew at her. Olivia ducked, and the others joined in —Carrie snorting into her drink, Lori rolling her eyes. For a moment it was just that: five women on a beach, giving each other a hard time.

"More chips?" Carrie held up the bag.

"Please," Jen said.

They passed the bag around. The afternoon stretched out —hours lost to the water, to naps in the chairs, to walks up the promenade for ice cream. By three the umbrellas started coming down around them. By four they'd packed up and made the slow walk back, everyone sun-tired and salt-sticky and ready for a shower.

The outdoor shower off the side gate ran for forty-five minutes straight. The teenagers cycled through first, loud and impatient, tracking sand across the deck and arguing about who'd been in there longest.

"Max, you've been in there for twenty minutes," Sophie yelled through the slats.

"I'm rinsing."

"You're stalling."

"I'm thinking."

"Think faster."

By the time the women took their turns, the sun was lower and the water pressure had recovered.

Meredith went last. The water was lukewarm now, but she

didn't mind. She could hear the others out by the pool—
splashing, voices, the clink of ice in glasses.

The pool filled up without anyone organizing it. The
teenagers claimed the water; the women took the middle deck
with their drinks. Carrie had found a bag of pretzels and put
them in a bowl. Lori had her feet up. Jen had the chair facing
the street, not the ocean.

"I could stay right here forever," Lori said.

"Until the hot tub's ready," Carrie said.

"Even better." Lori stretched her arms overhead.

Carrie threw a pretzel at her. Lori caught it and ate it.

Olivia's phone buzzed. She glanced at the screen—Dan—
then turned it face-down on the armrest.

"You can answer that," Jen said.

"It's fine." She didn't look up. "It's just Dan."

Nobody pushed. Carrie slid the pretzels toward Jen.

"I'm going to grab more water." Olivia stood and went
inside. Through the sliding door they could see her moving
through the kitchen, phone in hand now, then through the
living room and out of sight.

Jen's eyes followed her. So did Meredith's.

Inside, the trash was overflowing. Meredith dealt with it herself,
then wrote "trash" on the notepad she'd left on the counter that
morning. She called everyone together before dinner—"just a
quick thing"—and went through the chore chart she'd made
before they'd left home. Trash rotation, dishes, beach gear.

"Is this mandatory," Brittany asked from the doorway, "or
more of a vibe?"

"Mandatory," Meredith said.

"Got it. Just checking the vibe."

The chart went on the refrigerator. People drifted back to
wherever they'd been.

Lori stayed at the counter after the others had gone, fingers wrapped around a glass of water she wasn't drinking. "I keep thinking he'll snap out of it," she said, voice low. "But he's just getting further away."

Meredith leaned against the counter, listening.

"He used to talk to me," Lori said. "Before the divorce, even when things were bad, he'd still talk. Now it's like he's behind glass."

"He's angry."

"I know he's angry. I just don't know how to reach him through it."

"Maybe he needs to come to you."

"And if he doesn't?"

Meredith didn't have an answer. She wasn't sure there was one.

* * *

Carrie's laptop was open on the bed.

The spreadsheet had not changed since she'd last checked it—same columns, same numbers, same dread. Column A: fixed monthly. Column B: variable. Column C: what was left. That last column was what she kept returning to, as if the numbers might rearrange themselves into something less frightening.

She'd paid for her share of the hoagies without blinking. She'd brought the cheese board from Whole Foods that she hadn't needed and did not regret, mostly. Richard would have had something to say about all of it—Richard, who had managed their money for twenty years, who had left her with a house she couldn't quite afford and a future she couldn't quite see.

Divorce was math. Nobody warned you about that part. Lawyers and feelings, yes, but underneath all of it: math. What you had, what you owed, what was left when you divided everything in half and subtracted the cost of starting over.

Three more months. She just needed to keep the numbers from getting worse until then.

She stared at the ceiling.

Downstairs, she could hear the TV, footsteps moving through the kitchen, someone opening the refrigerator. Normal sounds. A house full of people going about their evening.

She shut the laptop, left it on the bed, and went downstairs.

* * *

The middle deck had emptied out except for Olivia, who sat with her phone face-up on the arm of her chair.

There was a text. Not from Dan.

How's the house? Thinking about you.

She read it. Read it again. The words were simple—friendly, even. Innocent, if you wanted them to be. But she knew what was underneath them, and she knew he did too.

The ocean moved in the dark below the dune. From somewhere inside she could hear the television, voices.

You're writing a book about it. That's what she had said to Jen at the beach. But wasn't Olivia writing something too? A story she was telling herself about why this was okay, why texting someone who wasn't her husband didn't count, why she could stand on this line without crossing it.

She typed a reply. Stopped. Deleted it.

Dan had texted too. *Hope you're having a good time. Miss you.*

Before February, that text would have made her smile. Now she didn't know what to do with it.

She didn't answer either of them.

The sliding door opened. Jen, with two glasses of wine.

"Thought you could use one."

Olivia took it. Jen leaned against the railing, looking out at the dark.

"It's not Dan," Olivia said. "The texts."

Jen didn't seem surprised. "I figured."

"How?"

"You check your phone like you're waiting for something good. That's not how people check for their husband."

Olivia drank from the glass. Jen was right.

"We don't have to talk about it," Jen said.

"Not tonight."

"Okay."

They stood there together, watching the pool lights shift on the water below.

"His name is Michael," Olivia said, barely audible.

Jen nodded and left it there.

* * *

Later, the house had gone quiet. Most of the teenagers were upstairs. The TV in the living room played to no one.

Jen had the couch to herself, laptop balanced on her knees.

Her editor's email was still there, still unanswered. Four days old now. *Just checking in on the draft, no pressure, but we're coming up on...*

She typed a sentence. Deleted it.

A summer away—that's what she'd told herself this was for. Fresh perspective, her agent had said, as if the problem were geography.

She thought about standing in the shallows that morning— the water around her ankles, the horizon line, how small it had made everything else feel.

She typed another sentence. Then another. Read them both.

Left them there.

Two sentences. She'd take it. She closed the laptop and sat with that small victory until her wine was gone.

* * *

In the converted sunroom at the back of the house, the lights were off. Max was already asleep, or pretending to be. Ethan lay on his bed with his earbuds in, something low and steady playing—not loud enough to hear the words, just the pulse of it.

He'd checked his phone twice since dinner. Nothing from any of the six places he'd applied. Not even a text. Sophie walked past a restaurant once and got an interview the next day. He'd walked in, filled out the applications, and heard nothing back.

Through the thin walls, he'd heard his mother's footsteps earlier—heard them stop outside the sunroom door and wait there, long enough that he knew she wanted to knock.

She didn't. That was what got him. She wanted to—he could practically feel it—but she didn't.

He didn't know if that made it better or worse.

His phone buzzed. His dad. *Hey bud, give me a call when you get a chance. Want to talk about the wedding stuff.*

Ethan read it then dropped the phone on the mattress beside him.

The music kept playing.

He closed his eyes and tried not to think about any of it.

* * *

By eleven, the noise had faded to murmurs.

The market lights along the pool fence swayed in a breeze that had come up off the ocean. Inside, the TV flickered blue and low.

On the rooftop, Meredith finished her wine and set the glass on the arm of her chair.

A whole summer. She'd made a chore chart, and nobody had refused to follow it—yet. She had a daughter leaving in

September and a husband back home running retirement numbers and her oldest friends all under the same roof, bringing their messes with them. They always had. That was the deal.

The first stars were out, bright and steady over the water.

She thought about what Olivia had said at the beach. What Carrie hadn't said. The way Lori kept watching Ethan like she could pull him back to her through sheer attention.

Everyone had brought something with them this summer. Suitcases and beach chairs and the kind of baggage that didn't fit in a car.

Somewhere below, she heard Lily laugh—sudden and easy—followed by Sophie, then Ava. The three of them finding something funny at eleven o'clock on the second night of vacation.

Meredith stayed where she was.

Tomorrow they'd figure out groceries. Tomorrow Sophie had her interview. Tomorrow Ethan would still be checking his phone, and Olivia would answer Dan's texts or she wouldn't, and Carrie would check her spreadsheet again and try not to let it show.

And Meredith would be watching. She always was. That was what it meant to be the one who organized—you saw everything, even the parts people thought they were hiding.

CHAPTER THREE

The promenade was different early in the morning.

Meredith had slipped out before anyone else was awake. She'd wanted the air. The stillness. The version of Sea Isle that existed before the beach crowds descended and the day demanded something from her.

At seven-thirty, the concrete path belonged to joggers and a few older couples moving slowly with their coffees. The shops were still shuttered, metal gates down, the gift shops and boutiques and bike rental places all waiting for the sun to climb higher. A man in a faded Phillies cap was hosing down the sidewalk in front of a breakfast place, and the smell of bacon drifted out through the propped-open door.

She passed someone unlocking the door of a surf shop, a stack of boogie boards visible through the window. Two women in visors power-walked past her, deep in conversation about someone's daughter-in-law. A city worker emptied a trash can near one of the benches, nodded at her, moved on to the next.

Two days in, and she was already remembering why she'd loved this place. Sea Isle had been part of her summers since she was a kid. Family vacations first, then college weekends with the girls after they'd all met at Rowan University, then the early years of marriage when she and Tom would rent a small place for a week in August. The town had changed, of course. New restaurants, fancier houses, the promenade more polished than it used to be. But underneath all of it, Sea Isle was still Sea Isle. The salt air, the sound of the waves, the particular way the morning light hit the concrete path. Some things you didn't forget.

She cut off the promenade and walked the block to Cafe 4109 on Landis. The line was short this early, just a couple ahead of her, and she ordered an iced coffee for herself. The barista was a college-aged girl with a nose ring and a tattoo of a wave on her wrist, and she made small talk while the espresso machine hissed.

"Here for the week?"

"The summer, actually."

The girl's eyebrows went up. "The whole summer? Nice."

Nice. Meredith supposed it was. She'd been planning this for so long that she'd stopped thinking about whether it was nice and started thinking about whether it was possible. Whether the house would work, whether the kids would get along, whether five women and six teenagers could share a space for three months without someone ending up in the ocean.

So far, so good. But it was only day three.

She took her coffee and headed back toward the house. More people out now. A family loading beach gear into a wagon. Two teenagers on bikes weaving between parked cars. A woman in running shorts stretching against a stop sign, earbuds in, oblivious to everything around her.

By the time she turned onto 59th Street, the house was awake.

* * *

Sophie was in the kitchen when Meredith came through the door, phone pressed to her ear, pacing the length of the island.

"Okay," she was saying. "Okay, great. I'll be there. Thank you so much."

She hung up and turned, face lit in a way Meredith hadn't seen since they'd arrived.

"I got it."

Meredith set her coffee on the counter. "The Crabby Catch?"

"Hostess. I go in for training tomorrow, then I start for real later this week." Sophie was already moving, grabbing her phone, probably to text Trevor, then stopping herself. "They said I could pick up extra shifts if I want. And the tips are good, apparently, even for hostesses, because people tip on their way out and—"

Meredith crossed to her and pulled her into a hug, the kind that Sophie usually squirmed out of but this time didn't.

"I'm proud of you," Meredith said.

"It's just a hostess job."

"It's your first real job. That matters."

Sophie pulled back, but she was smiling. "I have to figure out what to wear. They said black pants and a white shirt, but like, what kind of white shirt? There are a lot of kinds."

"We'll figure it out."

The others filtered in over the next twenty minutes, drawn by Sophie's excitement. Lori appeared from the hallway, still in her robe. Carrie came down from upstairs, hair wet from the shower. Jen wandered in from the deck, where she'd apparently been sitting with her laptop, though the screen was dark now.

Sophie told the story three more times, each version a little smoother than the last. By the third telling, she'd added details about the manager, a woman named Diane who'd been running the restaurant for fifteen years and had "a really good energy."

"What does that mean?" Brittany asked, appearing in the doorway with Ava behind her. "Good energy?"

"It means she's not going to yell at me," Sophie said.

"Low bar."

"It's a bar I appreciate."

Lily came down next, then Max, the two of them arguing about something that had happened in the pool last night that neither of them would fully explain. Olivia followed, phone in hand, expression guarded.

Ethan appeared last, tall and tanned from yesterday's beach day, hair still messy from sleep. He moved past the group to the Keurig and started a cup without saying anything.

"Sophie got the job," Lily announced, as if he hadn't heard it through the walls.

"Yeah, I heard." He leaned against the counter, waiting for the cup to fill. "Congrats."

Sophie looked at him. "Thanks."

"When do you start?"

"Tomorrow. Training first, then real shifts by the weekend."

He nodded. "That's cool. You'll be good at it."

And then, before anyone could ask him about his own search, he grabbed his coffee and headed for the back door. "I'm gonna go for a walk."

The screen door closed behind him.

* * *

By evening, they'd left the kids at the house and claimed a corner table at La Finestra.

It was BYOB, so Jen had brought two bottles of red. They'd snagged a table on the second floor, white linen, ocean views, their server opening the first bottle while they settled in.

Five women, midforties, taking up space like they'd earned it.

Lori sat across from Meredith. Tan and athletic now, transformed since the divorce. She'd cut her hair into a choppy bob, dyed it a shade darker, started running and lifting. Six months after Kevin left her for a trainer, she'd finally joined a gym. But it wasn't about him anymore. It was about reclaiming herself.

Olivia had that Mediterranean beauty. Dark hair, olive skin, expressive brown eyes. She'd dressed carefully tonight, a silk wrap dress in deep green, delicate gold hoops. She was the kind of woman men noticed, though she'd stopped noticing them noticing her years ago.

The first half of dinner was easy.

They talked about the menu, about someone's sunburn, about whether Lily would actually apply to ice cream shops. Light conversation that didn't require anything from anyone.

"Sophie seems happy," Olivia said, when the conversation turned to the kids.

"She's thrilled," Meredith said. "First job jitters, but the good kind."

"Lily's jealous," Olivia admitted. "She wants to find something too, but she's only fifteen."

"Ice cream shops hire at fifteen," Jen said.

"That's what I told her. She said ice cream is beneath her."

"Beneath her?"

"She's fifteen. Everything is beneath her."

They laughed again. The wine was poured, refilled, poured again. The conversation moved the way it did when you'd known each other long enough that silence wasn't awkward and no topic was off-limits.

Except that wasn't quite true anymore, was it? Somewhere along the way, updates had replaced real conversations. They knew the surface of each other's lives, but not what was underneath.

Then Carrie reached for the bread basket and said, almost to herself: "I should probably skip the lobster. Given, you know, everything."

It landed wrong.

Everyone went still. Jen stopped mid-bite. Lori looked up.

"I'm fine. I'm joking." Carrie's smile fell flat. "Really. I'm fine."

But she wasn't. And they all knew it.

They'd shared some of this at the beach yesterday. The affairs, the divorce, the engagement. Headlines. But sitting here now, leaning in over the noise of the crowded room, headlines weren't enough.

It started with Carrie, because she'd been the one to crack first, and once she did there was no point pretending everything was fine.

"You know Richard left," she said. "But I didn't tell you all of it. He left for Diana. His business partner." Carrie's fingers traced the stem of her wine glass, not drinking, just holding. "Except I was his business partner first. My idea, originally. Back when we were young and broke and didn't know anything about anything."

Carrie had done the books. Found the first clients. Built the whole thing alongside him until the girls came and someone had to be home. Richard promised it was temporary. That she'd come back once they were in school. But temporary stretched into years, and by the time she was ready to return, there was no room for her anymore.

"Then Diana came on five years ago. Smart. Capable." She looked down at her wine. "Younger. She'd been a client first, one Richard landed three years before she joined the company. I used to joke that she was his favorite, always laughing at his jokes, always requesting him specifically. Then he offered her the partnership that should have been mine."

Carrie tucked a strand of curly red hair behind her ear.

"She used to text him on weekends. Work stuff, supposedly. He'd be on his phone at Ava's soccer games, at dinner, in bed. I asked him about it once, and he said I was being paranoid. That Diana was like a little sister to him." She laughed, but there was nothing funny in it. "I found out later they'd been sleeping together for two years. Two years. While I was making her a Christmas gift basket. While she was coming to our Fourth of July barbecue and telling me how lucky Richard was to have me."

"The worst part?" She closed her eyes briefly. "I threw him a surprise party for his forty-fifth birthday last spring. Invited everyone from the office. Diana stood in my kitchen, drank my wine, handed him a gift she'd clearly spent too much time picking out. Six weeks later, he moved out."

The table went quiet.

"The divorce isn't even final yet. His lawyers keep delaying, finding reasons to push back the court date. Meanwhile I'm living off savings, waiting for a settlement that his attorney is trying to gut. He wants to argue that the business was his, that my contribution was minimal." Her voice hardened. "Twenty years of minimal contribution."

"You'll get what you're owed," Meredith said.

"Maybe. My lawyer says we have a strong case. But strong cases take time, and time costs money, and I've got about three months of savings left before I have to make some very hard decisions."

She hadn't told Brittany or Ava. Hadn't found a way to say it without making everything worse than it already was.

"I keep thinking I'll figure it out before I have to say anything," she said. "But I'm running out of time."

Lori put a hand on her shoulder. Nobody said anything for a long moment.

"At least you knew why," Lori said finally. "I spent a year thinking it was my fault."

The words hit hard. Lori had told them about the engagement, about Tessa. But not this.

Lori drained the rest of her wine and set the glass down with a thud. "Kevin said he needed to 'work on himself.' That's how he put it, back when things started to go wrong. Work on himself."

She'd believed him. Why wouldn't she? He was her husband.

"He started coming home later. Said he was doing extra sessions. Then he started criticizing everything—the way I cooked, the way I parented, the fact that I didn't have hobbies outside the house." She ran a finger around the rim of her empty glass. "He told me I was too negative. That I didn't support his growth. That I was holding him back from becoming the person he was meant to be."

Jen made a sound of disgust.

"I went to therapy," Lori said. "Tried to figure out what I was doing wrong. How to be less negative. How to support his journey, or whatever he called it." A bitter laugh escaped her. "Meanwhile, Tessa was posting workout videos on Instagram. And if you looked carefully—which I did, later, after I knew— Kevin was in the background of at least a dozen of them. Stretching. Spotting her. Once, his hand on her lower back."

"Before the divorce was even final?" Olivia asked.

"Before he even asked for one. Those videos were from when we were still trying. When I was reading self-help books and making his favorite dinners and wondering why nothing I did was ever enough."

She reached for the bottle and refilled her glass.

"I didn't know about her. Not until after the papers were signed, after the house was sold, after I'd spent a year thinking maybe the divorce was my fault." She took a breath. "Then I saw a photo on Kevin's Instagram. Him and Tessa on some hiking trail, her hand on his chest, both of them glowing. The caption said *Two years with this one.*"

Two years. The math wasn't hard.

"He was already gone," Lori said. "I just didn't know it yet."

And now Ethan had to stand up at the wedding. Be a groomsman. Smile for photos next to a woman who had been sleeping with his father while his parents were still married.

"The groomsman thing was Tessa's idea," Lori added. "She wants the 'blended family' photo op. Told Kevin it would show everyone they're all moving forward together. Like she's not the reason we fell apart."

"Ethan hasn't said yes. He hasn't said no. He just... stopped talking. Stopped coming out of his room, stopped answering Kevin's calls. He was already angry about the divorce, and now this."

Meredith leaned forward. "Can you tell him he doesn't have to do it?"

"I want to. Every day I want to." Lori pressed her fingers to her temples. "But if I do, I'm the bitter ex-wife. I'm the reason he doesn't have a relationship with his dad. Kevin's already told Ethan that I poisoned him against the idea. That I can't let go. That I'm the toxic one." She paused. "I can't be that mother. I won't."

She stared at the ceiling for a moment, composing herself.

"So I just watch him disappear. Watch him carry all this anger he doesn't know what to do with. And I can't fix it because anything I say gets twisted into proof that I'm the problem."

Olivia had been listening through Carrie and Lori's confessions, arms crossed, staring at the table. But now she spoke.

Dan. The emotional affair. The texts. The counseling. They'd heard the outline at the beach. Not what she'd actually seen.

"February," she said. "A Tuesday. I came home from work early because I had a headache. Dan was in the shower. His phone was on the kitchen counter, and it lit up with a text."

The name said Rachel. A coworker. Olivia had met her once at a holiday party. Nice enough. Forgettable.

"The text said: *I wish I could talk to you right now.*"

Olivia had picked up the phone. She didn't mean to. She just did.

"There were hundreds of messages. Months of them." Her

voice caught. "Not sexual. That was the thing. No photos, no explicit language. Just... intimacy."

Inside jokes. Complaints about their days. Conversations Dan should have been having with her.

You're the only one who gets it. I hate that we can't just be together. I think about you constantly.

"He didn't sleep with her," Olivia said. "At least he says he didn't. But he was hers. Emotionally, completely hers."

The confrontation. The tears. Dan swearing it was over, he'd made a mistake, he'd do anything. Couples counseling. Date nights. The whole playbook.

"And I'm supposed to forgive him," Olivia said. "Because he didn't technically cross the line."

She stopped there. No one moved.

"But I might."

No one knew what to say to that.

"There's someone," Olivia said. "His name is Michael. I joined a hiking group a few months ago, just to get out of the house. To have something that was mine." She looked toward the window, the dark ocean beyond. "We started carpooling to the trailheads. Just logistics at first. Then we'd grab coffee after. Then the coffee turned into lunch."

It had started as venting. He was divorced, understood what it was like to feel alone inside a marriage. He listened to her. Really listened. Something Dan hadn't done in years.

"I haven't done anything. We haven't..." She stopped. "It's not like that. But I think about him. I check my phone for his texts. I get dressed more carefully on hiking days. I..."

She couldn't finish.

"I'm standing on the line," she said. "And I don't know which way I'm going to fall."

"Whatever you decide," Jen said, "you're not doing it alone."

The others murmured agreement.

Carrie leaned forward, elbows on the table. Maybe to lighten the mood, maybe because it felt like her turn.

"Okay," she said to Jen. "Your turn. What's your damage?"

Jen gave a short laugh. "My damage. Where do I start?" She pushed up the sleeves of her blouse, revealing the tattoos she'd started collecting in her thirties. A line of poetry on her left forearm, a small moth on her wrist, a half-sleeve of wildflowers she was still adding to. Her bleached-blond hair fell in a shaggy, layered cut that grazed her shoulders, a style that looked effortless but probably wasn't. Angular face, sharp cheekbones, silver rings stacked on her fingers. She was the one who'd never looked like the rest of them, even back at Rowan —always a little more interesting, a little harder to pin down.

"No affair. No divorce." She shrugged. "Just twenty years of waiting for something that never showed up."

She'd told them about deleting the apps. Said she was done looking. David, too—three years in her early thirties, the one who'd wanted to get married. But she'd never said why she ended it.

"I panicked." She touched the moth tattoo on her wrist. "Told myself he wasn't right, that something was missing, that I needed more time to figure out what I wanted." She paused. "So I ended it. Moved to a new city. Threw myself into work."

"What happened to him?" Olivia asked.

"Married someone else within two years. Three kids now. Looks happy in every photo I've ever accidentally seen." Jen exhaled. "I spent a long time telling myself I made the right call. That I would've been miserable. But honestly? I think I was just scared. And by the time I figured that out, it was too late."

She let it sit.

"Last month I went out with a guy who seemed perfect on paper. Divorced, no kids, runs his own architecture firm. Great texts. We met for dinner, and within ten minutes he's telling me how *refreshing* I am." She made air quotes. "He said he doesn't usually date women his own age. That most of them are too bitter, too desperate, too much baggage. But I seemed *different*."

"Unbelievable," Lori muttered.

"It gets better. He asked me—over appetizers—why I'd never been married. Said there must be something wrong with me if I'd made it to forty-five without anyone locking it down." A dry laugh. "Locking it down. Like I'm a car that keeps failing inspection."

"Please tell me you walked out," Carrie said.

"I should have. Instead I sat through the whole dinner because I'd already ordered the salmon and I was hungry." She rolled her eyes. "He texted the next day saying he had a great time and asking when he could see me again. No self-aware-ness. None."

"And before that?" Meredith asked.

"Before that was the guy who cried about his ex-wife for two hours. Before that was the one who asked if I'd ever considered freezing my eggs, 'just in case.' Before that was the investment banker who spent the whole dinner on his phone and then got offended when I didn't want a second date." She picked at the edge of her napkin. "I kept thinking: next year. Next app. Next city. Next version of myself. And then I turned forty-five and realized I'd spent my whole adult life in a waiting room."

"For what?" Lori asked.

"For my life to start."

She shrugged, playing it off, but she wasn't fooling anyone.

"So I deleted the apps. I decided I'm done waiting. If it happens, it happens. If it doesn't, I have a book to write and a cat who tolerates me."

Olivia looked up. "How's the book going?"

Jen's mouth twitched.

"It's going," she said.

That was all. But they'd known her long enough to hear what she wasn't saying.

Eyes turned to Meredith.

She'd been the listener all night. The one asking the hard questions, absorbing everyone else's confessions. Now it was her turn.

"What about you?" Carrie said.

Meredith reached for her wine. "I'm fine. Tom's fine. We're fine."

A beat. Meredith smoothed the napkin in her lap, buying time.

The retirement plan. Him home all the time. She'd touched on it at the beach. But they were waiting for more.

"We've been married for twenty-three years. And I love him. I do." Her voice was steady, but there was something she wasn't letting all the way out. "But we've always had space. Work, kids, separate rhythms. I don't know what we are without that."

"And that scares you," Jen said.

"No. I don't know. Maybe."

She looked down at her hands. Put the mask back on.

"It's not like what you're all dealing with. It's fine. I'm being dramatic."

The others didn't push. They knew her. She wasn't ready to go further.

But she'd said more than she meant to. And Meredith knew it, even as she signaled for the check.

* * *

The promenade had emptied out, the dinner crowds thinned to couples and the occasional group of teenagers with places to be.

They spilled out of La Finestra arm in arm, heels in hands by the second block. The night air had cooled, touched with the faint char of someone's grill. The ocean was right there beyond the dunes, dark and steady, the sound of the waves a constant underneath everything else.

Someone laughed at nothing. Someone else joined.

"We're disasters," Carrie said.

"Complete disasters," Lori agreed.

"We're fine," Jen said.

"We're not fine," Olivia countered.

"We're something," Meredith said.

They walked. Past the ice cream shops with their late-night lines and the quiet houses, the ocean somewhere beyond them, audible but unseen.

The house came into view at the end of 59th Street. Lit up from inside, every window bright. Voices carried through the screens. Lily's laugh, the muffled thump of music, Max yelling something that might have been "That doesn't count!"

They paused where the sidewalk met the yard. Looked at each other.

Then they went inside, peeling off one by one. Someone headed for the kitchen for water. Someone else for the bathroom. Someone straight upstairs to bed, heels still in hand, not bothering to say goodnight.

CHAPTER FOUR

By mid-morning, the group had scattered. Some at the beach, some around town, everyone carving out their own corner of the day.

Lily was stretched out on a towel, texting, occasionally smiling at her phone. Max had joined a pickup volleyball game down the beach, jumping for a spike, missing, laughing it off. Ava sat a little apart, sketchbook open, working on something she kept angled away from everyone. Meredith had a book open but wasn't reading it.

Olivia dug through her beach bag and pulled out a pair of swim goggles—not the cheap drugstore kind, but real ones, competition-grade. She'd been on the team at Rowan, back before Dan and the twins and everything that came after. She still swam laps at the community pool when she could find the time, which wasn't often enough.

But this was different. This was the ocean.

She stood, brushed sand off her legs, and pulled her hair back into a tight ponytail.

"Going in?" Meredith asked.

"Going to swim."

She walked toward the shoreline without waiting for a

response. She didn't stop at the shallows. Didn't ease in. She waded until the water hit her thighs, then dove under and started swimming—real swimming, with form and purpose, arms slicing through the water in clean strokes.

The cold hit her like a reset. She surfaced, adjusted her goggles, and kept going, out past the breakers, into the deep blue where the swells lifted her up and set her back down.

Her shoulders burned. Her lungs burned. It felt good. Pain that meant something was happening.

She swam parallel to the coastline for what felt like forever, past the lifeguard stand, past the next beach entrance, maybe four or five blocks before she finally turned back. The swells were gentle on the return, and she let herself bob over them, arms loose, catching her breath between strokes.

When she made her way back to the sand, her legs were shaky and her muscles were singing. She dropped onto her towel and lay there, chest heaving, eyes closed, face tilted toward the sun.

"Feel good?" Meredith asked.

"Yeah." Olivia didn't open her eyes. "It really did."

She'd been a professor since her early thirties, art history at a small college outside Philadelphia, specializing in nineteenth-century American painters. She loved it, the teaching and the research, the students who occasionally caught fire over the same things she did. But somewhere along the way, the job had become obligation instead of passion. Office hours, committee meetings, recommendation letters, the endless grading. She couldn't remember the last time she'd done something purely for herself.

This. This had been that.

She reached for her phone out of habit, the habit she was trying to break, the one where she checked it every few minutes as if the world couldn't wait.

Three texts from Dan. The first casual: Hope you're having fun. The second slightly less so: Call me when you get a chance? The third with an edge she could hear even through the screen: Starting to feel like you're avoiding me.

She was. She knew she was.

One text from Michael: Good morning. Hope the ocean is treating you well.

Her stomach flipped. A flutter, a lift, a charge she hadn't felt toward Dan in years. Michael knew she was married, knew it was complicated. He probably thought she was on her way out.

Maybe she was.

She looked at Dan's messages again. Starting to feel like you're avoiding me. The audacity of it almost made her laugh. He'd spent months texting another woman, pouring himself into someone else's inbox, and now he wanted to know why she wasn't calling him back?

She typed a reply: At the beach. Kids are good. Talk later.

She didn't reply to Michael. Not yet.

She set the phone face-down on the towel beside her. Her shoulders ached in that good way, muscles remembering what they used to do. The pool at home was fine, but the ocean was something else. Open water, salt, the pull of the current. Her body still knew how.

Max came jogging up from the volleyball game, sweaty and grinning. He dropped onto the corner of Lily's towel. She kicked at him until he moved.

"We won," he said. "Three games straight."

"Nobody cares."

"You're just mad because you haven't moved in two hours."

Lily didn't dignify that with a response.

* * *

Sophie arrived at The Crabby Catch ten minutes before her training shift.

She'd agonized over the outfit—black pants, white button-down, exactly what Diane had described—and then second-guessed whether the button-down was too formal, changed into a different white shirt, changed back. Brittany had finally thrown a pillow at her and told her to pick one and leave.

The restaurant was already in motion. Through the front windows, Sophie could see servers folding napkins and someone hauling a crate of produce toward the kitchen. She pushed through the door and found Diane at the hostess stand, marking up a clipboard.

"Sophie. Good." Diane set the clipboard aside. "Let's walk through everything."

The training was more involved than Sophie had expected. The iPad system for check-ins, the waitlist protocol, how to handle incomplete parties who insisted on being seated, how to smile at difficult guests without actually conceding anything. Diane covered it all with the precision of someone who'd trained dozens of new hires.

"Questions?" Diane asked, when they'd finished the basics.

"Where are the backup menus? In case I run out during a rush."

"Smart." Diane gestured down the back hallway. "Storage room, past the kitchen. Jake can show you."

She flagged down a guy who'd just finished taking an order at a nearby table. He tucked his notepad into his apron and walked over. Sandy-blond hair, a small scar through one eyebrow, moving like someone who'd worked here long enough to know every shortcut.

"Jake, this is Sophie. New hostess. Can you show her where the supplies are?"

"Yeah, sure." He wiped his hands on his apron. "Follow me."

Sophie followed him through the dining room, past the kitchen door where someone was yelling about shrimp, and into a narrow hallway lined with metal shelving.

"Menus here," Jake said, pointing. "Napkins, tablecloths,

candles there. Extra silverware in that bin." He gestured to a locked cabinet at the end. "That's liquor. You won't touch it."

"Thanks." Sophie grabbed a stack of menus.

"No problem." He turned to go then paused. "You here all summer?"

"Yeah. My mom rented a house with friends. Big group of us on 59th."

"Nice. I'm here every summer. Grandparents live year-round, so I've been coming down since I was a kid. Started bussing at fourteen. Now I'm saving up for recording equipment." He rubbed the back of his neck. "Music stuff. Probably sounds dumb."

"It doesn't."

He looked at her for a second, like he was deciding whether she meant it. "Anyway. Diane's demanding, but fair. You'll be fine."

He headed back to the dining room, and Sophie returned to the hostess stand, sliding the menus into the basket. Checking through the reservation system, she heard the front door open. Ethan walked in.

His arrival surprised her. He looked like he hadn't expected to be there either, shoulders drawn up, hands in his pockets, eyes looking for somewhere else to land.

"Hey," Sophie said. "What are you doing here?"

"Callback." He crossed his arms, uncrossed them. "Busboy."

"Ethan, that's great."

"It's clearing plates." He shrugged.

"It's a paycheck."

His expression loosened. Not a smile, but close.

Diane appeared from the back. "Ethan? You're the eleven o'clock?"

"Yeah."

"Come on back. We'll talk in the office."

He followed her to the bar area. Sophie turned to the iPad. Jake passed by with a tray of drinks, heading for the patio.

"Friend of yours?" he asked.

"Sort of. Family friends. Our moms are friends. We're all staying in the same house."

"Ah." He looked back at the office door. "He seems nervous."

"He's been applying since we got here. Starting to get in his head about it."

Jake nodded. "He'll get it. Diane likes people who show up early."

He walked off toward the patio.

Her phone buzzed. Trevor.

Thinking about you. How's the first day?

She typed back: Learning a lot. Call you tonight?

Can't wait.

She slid it back into her bag.

Trevor was an hour and a half away. Steady, uncomplicated, exactly what she'd wanted when she'd agreed to spend the summer apart. But he was also texts and calls and a face on a screen, held in her hand instead of standing next to her.

On the patio, Jake was taking an order, leaning in with a grin that made the table laugh. Recording equipment. Music stuff. The scar through his eyebrow.

Sophie turned back to the reservation screen. Opened the next hour's bookings. Focused.

Then Ethan emerged from the back, face giving nothing away.

"Well?"

"I start Thursday." He didn't quite smile, but his shoulders dropped an inch.

"That's amazing."

"It's clearing plates," he said, but he was almost smiling.

"It's a start." She punched his arm. "Your mom's going to be thrilled."

For a second, it looked like he might let himself feel it. Then he looked away. "Yeah. I guess."

He left through the front door, and Sophie turned to her station. Ten minutes until her first real shift. Menus to organize, a system to master, a whole summer stretching ahead.

She was ready.

* * *

The coffee shop on Landis was called Driftwood Coffee, and Jen had claimed a table by the window with her laptop and a determination to actually work.

An iced latte sweated beside her laptop, and she'd already eaten half of the blueberry scone she'd grabbed at the counter. If she was going to take up space for hours, she might as well contribute to the local economy.

The cozy mystery was open—the one her editor had been asking about, stuck at seventy-five percent and stalled for three months. Six of these books behind her. Quirky sleuth, small town, body in the first chapter, suspects with secrets, resolution by page three hundred.

She read the last paragraph she'd written. Then read it again.

A sentence. Another. A third.

Highlighted. Deleted.

Her fingers found the new document button before she'd made a conscious decision.

Just to clear her head, she told herself. To shake loose whatever was stuck.

And something else entirely poured out.

A woman facing a forest that shouldn't exist, rising where the field abruptly ended. Two moons overhead, one silver, one the color of old copper. Magic that moved through the trees like water, visible if you knew how to look. The woman didn't know how to look, not yet, but she could feel it against her skin, waiting to be noticed.

And then, inevitably, a man appeared. Dark-haired, sharp-tongued, saying one thing and meaning three others. He stepped out of the tree line like he'd been waiting for her, which he probably had.

The sentences came faster than they had in months. Page one became page two became page three, and when Jen finally looked up, an hour had passed.

She went to the counter for another iced latte. The barista smiled like she recognized a fellow creative mid-breakthrough. Jen took her drink back to the table and kept writing.

Scrolling back to the beginning revealed three pages of work that felt nothing like obligation.

Not the book she was supposed to write. Not even the genre. Her agent repped cozy mysteries. Her brand was tea and cats and bodies discovered in quaint village settings. And yet here it was—romance and magic and a world she hadn't known was waiting.

She saved the file. Named it "DON'T DELETE" because she knew herself well enough.

She was still looking at the document when she felt someone watching her.

A scan of the coffee shop, and she found him immediately.

Corner table, near the back. Brown hair that needed cutting, stubble that suggested forgetfulness rather than style. Laptop open, coffee cup long empty, a paperback splayed face-down beside him, a sci-fi novel with a spaceship on the cover. He wore a faded T-shirt with a logo too cracked to read, what might have been a venue name once. His fingers moved across the keyboard in bursts—urgent, then stopping, then starting again. Between bursts, he'd pick up his phone and tap at it, or stare at the screen like he was trying to hear something that wasn't there. Then back to typing. Then the paperback—a few lines, set it back down. A reset.

When he paused, his eyes swept the room. Found her.

Jen looked away first. Pretended to read her screen. But she kept tracking him from the corner of her eye. She noticed his hands, long fingers, calluses at the tips.

He was back to typing. Whatever he was working on had him the same way her new document had her—consumed, struggling, racing to capture it before it disappeared.

The "DON'T DELETE" file. Another paragraph. Then another.

The man in the corner kept typing.

Two more hours passed. When she packed up to leave, he was still there, coffee cup finally refilled, paperback now closed, posture looser than before.

Their eyes met as she passed his table. He raised two fingers off the laptop, a small salute, the kind you give a fellow traveler. She returned it.

No words exchanged.

But Jen left knowing she'd be back at that table tomorrow. And wondering if he would too.

* * *

Carrie arrived at the farmer's market as vendors were starting to pack up.

Excursion Park had transformed for the morning. Tents lined up along the paths, the late-morning crowd already thinning as noon approached.

She wandered through what remained. Strawberries picked up and put back, picked up again. Lettuce she didn't need, radishes she'd never cook with, a jar of local honey that caught her eye.

At the far end, one tent was still fully set up. Saltmeadow Farm, the hand-painted sign read. Wooden crates of vegetables in neat rows. Behind the table stood a woman around sixty—

silver hair in a loose braid, dirt under her nails, deep tan lines at her collar.

"Still shopping?" the woman asked as Carrie approached.

"Just looking. I think I overbought at the other tables."

The woman laughed. "Happens to everyone. First market of the season?"

"First for me."

A satisfied nod. "You'll learn the rhythm. Different things come into season as the weeks go by. July, you'll want the tomatoes and corn. August, the peppers and melons."

Carrie picked up a zucchini, dark green and firm, smaller than the supermarket kind. "These are gorgeous."

"Best time of year for them." The woman leaned against the tent post. "I'm Marge. My husband and I started the farm forty years ago. He's back loading the truck. We're the last ones here most weeks."

"I'm Carrie."

"You look like you needed to get out of the house." Marge said it matter-of-factly, no judgment.

Carrie laughed, surprised. "Is it that obvious?"

"I've been doing this a long time. You learn to read people." Marge started bagging the zucchini. "If you want a break while you're here—somewhere to get out of your own head—we do tours of the farm. Nothing fancy. Walk through the fields, see how things grow. Some people find it grounding."

"That sounds nice."

"Come alone or bring people. Either way." A scrap of paper with an address and phone number. Marge handed it over with the bag. "Hope I see you out there."

Carrie made her way through the emptying market, produce in one hand, Marge's address in her pocket.

The farm. Twenty minutes inland, away from the beach and the house. A place where things grew because someone had planted and tended and waited.

Maybe she'd go.

* * *

Lori found the bookstore by accident.

She'd been walking without destination.

Tidewater Books sat between a fudge shop and a place selling beach chairs, easy to miss. The windows held summer reading displays: beaches and lighthouses and women in flowing dresses gazing at oceans.

Inside, it smelled like old paper and dried herbs. Shelves packed floor to ceiling, organized with what seemed either careful curation or cheerful chaos. A handwritten sign near the front said Fiction A-M and pointed left.

She started in fiction and lost track of time.

Books came off shelves, first pages got read, most went back. She wasn't searching for anything specific.

"Can I help you find anything?"

A man at the end of the aisle, watching her with genuine curiosity rather than retail obligation. Early fifties, thick hair in a ponytail that somehow worked. Faded Fleetwood Mac T-shirt. Glasses he pushed up his nose while waiting for her answer.

"Just browsing," Lori said.

"Best way to do it." He smiled and didn't leave. Instead, he stepped closer, scanning the spines near where she'd been browsing. "What have you been gravitating toward?"

"A little of everything." She held up the book in her hand, a woman on the cover walking into fog. "This one caught my eye."

He tilted his head to read the title. "Beautiful sentences in that one. Not much plot, takes its time. Some people find it slow."

"And you?"

"I loved it." He reached past her and slid another book from the shelf. "But if you want more momentum—this. Same depth, quicker pace. The ending stayed with me for weeks."

Lori looked at the cover. A house half-swallowed by ivy, a single lit window.

"I haven't heard of this."

"Small press, came out last year. The author did a reading here." He tapped the spine. "I try to stock things you won't find at the airport."

"Is that your niche?"

"One of them." He extended his hand. "John. I own the place."

"Lori."

"Take your time, Lori. I'll be up front if you need me."

He returned to the register, and Lori watched him go.

The usual retail exchange—forced cheer, the upsell, transaction dressed as conversation—she'd been ready for that. This hadn't been that. He'd been curious without agenda. Genuinely interested.

Another half hour of wandering, books accumulating in her arms. When she brought them to the register, John was finishing with another customer.

He turned to her. "Solid choices."

"You're persuasive."

"Occupational hazard." He scanned the books, movements calm and measured. "If you're around, I host a speaker series. Local voices—authors, historians, anyone with a good story about this place. Next one's later this week."

"I might check that out."

"You should. It's usually a full house."

Lori took the bag. "Thanks for the recommendations."

"Anytime."

She walked out into the afternoon.

* * *

The beach club was exactly what Brittany had expected—white lounge chairs in precise rows, a pool that belonged in a magazine, a bar serving twenty-dollar smoothies to people who didn't flinch at the price.

Her job was front desk and cabana rentals. Check members in, answer questions, maintain the smile. She'd worked a juice bar, a summer doing register at a boutique, but the beach club operated on different rules. These weren't customers. They were members. The distinction mattered here.

A few hours in, she was logging a rental when someone spoke up beside her.

"First day's always the longest."

The bartender. He set a bottle of water on the counter. "Figured you could use this."

"Thanks." She took it. "Brittany."

"Ryan." He leaned against the edge. "Let me guess. You're questioning all your life choices and wondering why you signed up for this."

She laughed. "Is it written on my face?"

"Everyone has that look their first day. It fades by week two." He gestured at the pool deck. "Members seem intimidating, but most of them just want to feel important. Treat them like they matter and they tip well."

"Noted."

A woman in oversized sunglasses approached and asked about the spa schedule, her tone suggesting Brittany should already know. Brittany smiled, found the answer, delivered it calmly. The woman left without thanking her.

Ryan watched her go. "Mrs. Everett. Never tips over ten percent and once sent back a margarita because the salt was 'uneven.'"

Brittany snorted. "Uneven salt."

"I wish I was kidding." He straightened up. "You handled that well, though. She's not easy."

"Customer service isn't new to me. Just the clientele."

"That's the trick." He started back toward the bar. "Same skills, different tax bracket."

The rest of the shift passed in a blur of check-ins and questions and the constant effort of keeping her face pleasant. But it felt slightly less impossible than it had that morning.

When she grabbed her bag to leave, Ryan was restocking glasses behind the bar. He looked up, met her gaze, and raised his water bottle. Same way he'd brought her one earlier. A callback.

She gave a small nod and headed out.

* * *

Tom's car was in the driveway.

Meredith sat for a moment, groceries in the passenger seat, trying to figure out what she felt.

She'd been out most of the afternoon. Grocery store, wine shop on Landis, a stop for batteries they probably didn't need. She'd still bought groceries for the house, but no one had texted her a list, no one had asked what time dinner would be ready. Just her, moving through a day.

And now Tom was here, three days early, without warning.

She grabbed the grocery bags and headed inside.

The living room was crowded. Sophie perched on the sectional arm, beaming. Jen leaning in the kitchen doorway. And at the island, grinning like he'd just executed a heist, was Tom.

"Hey, stranger." He crossed to her and took the bags. "Surprise."

She hugged him. "Why didn't you tell me? How long can you stay?"

"Weekend at least. Maybe longer if things stay quiet." He kissed her forehead. "Moved some showings around. You've been handling the contracts and listings from here, so I figured the team could spare me for a few days."

Sophie launched into a recap of her first day—Diane, the training, the reservation system, the news that Ethan had gotten hired at the same restaurant. Tom listened, asked questions, laughed where appropriate. He slipped into the space without effort, as he always did.

The evening unfolded easily. Pizza from DeNunzio's, eaten on the deck while the sky cycled through its colors. The teenagers scattered to their corners of the house. The adults lingered with drinks, conversation moving comfortably among people who knew each other well.

Tom sat beside Meredith on the loveseat, his hand on her knee. A story about work—a client who'd lowballed an offer, then acted shocked when the sellers countered at full ask—and everyone was laughing.

Meredith laughed too. She'd always been able to do that, even when her mind was elsewhere.

* * *

Later, after the deck emptied and Meredith stood alone at the railing, she let herself feel what she'd pushed down since walking through the door.

She'd been different here. Easier. She hadn't realized how much until Tom appeared in the kitchen and she felt herself pulling back into the familiar shape.

She loved him. That wasn't in question.

What unsettled her was harder to name. A restlessness she couldn't explain. Someone she'd started becoming here, in these few days, who didn't quite fit the contours of her marriage.

The pool glowed below. Beyond the dunes, the ocean kept its steady pull. Inside, Tom was asking Carrie about the farmer's market, his voice drifting through the screen door.

Meredith stayed at the railing until her breathing slowed.

It didn't disappear entirely. She hadn't expected it to.

She went inside. Kissed her husband. Pretended she wasn't still trying to understand what any of it meant.

CHAPTER FIVE

The address Marge had given her led inland, away from the salt air and the endless blue, through streets that traded beach houses for gas stations and shopping plazas before opening into something else entirely. Farmland. Actual farmland, twenty minutes from the ocean, stretching flat and green under the morning sky.

Saltmeadow Farm announced itself with a hand-painted sign at the entrance and rows of vegetables running in long parallel lines toward a red barn in the distance. An old split-rail fence marked the boundary between the dirt road and the fields beyond.

Carrie turned off the engine and sat for a moment, wondering what she was doing here.

The girls hadn't wanted to come. Brittany had an after-noon shift at the beach club and was using the morning to sleep in. Ava had barely looked up from the book she'd been reading on the deck—some fantasy novel with a cracked spine that she'd already made it halfway through, her camera resting on the chair beside her. "I'm good," she'd said, and that had been that. Carrie had learned not to push.

So she'd come alone. Which was maybe the point.

Inside the farm's entrance, a wooden stand displayed jars of honey and bundles of herbs tied with twine. A mutt lifted its head from a patch of shade, assessed Carrie as non-threatening, and lowered it again.

Beyond the stand, the farm opened up. Rows and rows of vegetables stretched toward the tree line—leafy greens in one section, tomato plants staked and heavy with fruit in another, squash vines sprawling across the soil. A pair of white hoop houses stood to the left, their plastic sides rolled up to let the breeze through, and beyond them a greenhouse with fogged glass caught the morning light. To the right, a red barn anchored the property, its doors thrown open to reveal stacked crates and the organized chaos of a working farm. A chicken coop sat beside it, and a dozen hens pecked at the dirt nearby, unbothered by anything. The whole place smelled like soil and growth, and Carrie couldn't remember the last time she'd slowed down enough to notice.

Near the greenhouse, a woman in rubber boots and a straw hat was loading crates onto a flatbed cart.

"Carrie?" The woman straightened, tipped back her hat. It was Marge, braid tucked over one shoulder, dirt on her knees. "You came."

"I came." Carrie was still taking it in—the scope of it, the life everywhere she looked. "This is incredible."

"Still surprises me some days." Marge wiped her hands on her jeans and gestured for Carrie to follow. "Let me show you around."

They walked the perimeter first. Up close, the farm revealed itself in layers. Marge pointed out the shaded beds where lettuce and arugula thrived in the cooler soil, the drip lines running between pepper plants, the marigolds planted at the end of each row to keep the pests away. She explained the rotation schedule, the irrigation system her husband Frank had rigged up thirty years ago that still worked better than anything modern, the way certain plants protected others when you put them side by side. Companion planting, she called it. Carrie liked the sound of that.

"Most people think farming is about putting seeds in the ground and waiting," Marge said, stopping beside a row of pepper plants heavy with fruit. "It's not. It's about paying attention. Reading what the soil tells you, what the leaves tell you. The plants will show you what they need if you know how to look."

Carrie crouched down and touched one of the pepper leaves. It was smooth and firm, almost waxy. "How do you learn that? To read them?"

"Time. Patience. Getting it wrong and trying again." Marge plucked a pepper—deep red, perfect—and handed it to Carrie. "You married?"

The question landed without warning. Carrie turned the pepper over in her hands. "I was. Divorced. Six months ago."

"Ah." Marge nodded like this explained something. "That's the look, then."

"What look?"

"The one where you're working out who you are now that you're not who you were." She started walking again, and Carrie fell into step beside her. "I've seen it before. People come to the farm when they're untethered. Dirt and growing things —they help."

They reached the greenhouse, and Marge pulled open the door. Inside, the air was thick and humid, carrying the green smell of things pushing toward life. Seedling trays lined metal shelving units, each one labeled in Marge's handwriting— Sunflowers, 6/10. Fall kale, 6/15. Zinnias—farmers market.

"This is where it starts," Marge said. "Everything out there began in here. Little plastic cells, handful of soil, one seed at a time."

Carrie moved between the rows, brushing her fingers over the trays. So much potential, contained in something so small. "Do they all make it?"

"No. Some don't germinate. Some get too much water or not enough sun. Some just don't take." Marge shrugged. "You plant twice what you need and hope for the best. Can't control everything."

Can't control everything. Carrie thought about the spreadsheet on her laptop, the columns of numbers that never seemed to add up no matter how many times she ran them. The house she'd shared with Richard for twenty years, the one she couldn't afford to keep on her own. The settlement negotiations that dragged on while his lawyers found new ways to minimize her contributions to a business she'd helped build from nothing. Even this vacation—they'd booked it back in January, when she still had access to the joint account and a future that looked different.

She'd spent her whole marriage trying to hold it together. Look where it got her.

"You want to help out while you're here?" Marge was watching her with that knowing look again. "We're potting up sunflower starts for the market today. Extra hands are always welcome."

"I don't know what I'm doing."

"Nobody does at first. That's the whole point of doing."

Carrie looked at her hands—clean, manicured, the nails she'd gotten done before leaving because that's what she did before vacations, before the life she used to have. She thought about getting dirt under them. The idea should have seemed beneath her—Richard's voice in her head, always Richard's voice, telling her that physical labor was for people who didn't have better options.

But Richard wasn't here. And his voice could go straight to wherever voices like that belonged.

"Show me what to do," Carrie said.

They spent the next two hours in the greenhouse. Marge demonstrated the technique first—how to ease the seedlings from their cells without damaging the roots, how to create a small depression in the soil of the pot, how to settle the plant and firm the soil around it without compressing too tightly. Carrie watched then tried it herself. Her first few attempts were clumsy, the seedlings listing to one side or the soil too loose. But Marge corrected her, adjusted her grip, showed her again.

By the fifth transplant, Carrie had found a rhythm. By the twentieth, she'd stopped thinking about Richard entirely.

The work was meditative—the repetition, the focus required, the way the world narrowed to this one small task. Lift, place, settle, firm. Move to the next. An exhaust fan droned at the far end of the greenhouse, pulling the humid air through but not doing much against the heat. Her shoulders ached from leaning over the table. Her fingers were caked with soil, and sweat dampened her hairline. And for the first time in longer than she could remember, her mind was quiet.

Frank appeared around noon with sandwiches and lemonade. He was a big man with a farmer's tan that stopped abruptly at his shirt sleeves, a faded Grateful Dead T-shirt stretched across his chest, and dirt permanently embedded in the creases of his knuckles. He set the tray on an overturned crate and nodded at Carrie like she'd been coming here for years.

"New recruit?" he asked Marge.

"That depends." Marge sat on a stool and reached for a sandwich, looking at Carrie. "You having a good time, or is this torture?"

Carrie laughed. "Honestly? Best morning I've had in months."

"Well then." Marge took a bite. "We hire part-time in the summer. Market setup, harvest days, whatever needs doing. Nothing glamorous. Fifteen dollars an hour plus produce. If you're interested."

"I wasn't—" Carrie started, then stopped. What was she going to say? That she hadn't come here looking for a job? That she was just a divorced woman from the suburbs who'd wandered into a farm because she didn't know what else to do with herself?

Except. Fifteen dollars an hour wouldn't make a dent in her financial problems. But it was something. And more than that—it was purpose. A reason to get up. A place where nobody knew her story, where she was a woman learning something new with soil on her hands.

"I'll think about it," Carrie said.

"Door's open whenever you want it." Marge bit into her sandwich. "We're here every day. Except Sundays. Sundays we rest."

After lunch, Carrie helped carry the potted seedlings to the shade structure where they'd harden off before market day. Then Frank waved her over to the tomato rows. The sun was higher now, the air hazy with June heat, but she didn't mind.

He showed her how to check the plants for signs of stress—yellowing leaves, spots that indicated fungus, fruit that wasn't developing right. He pointed to each problem silently then moved to the next plant. A man of few words, but the lesson was clear.

Carrie thought about all the years she'd pretended. Smiling at Diana across the table at company dinners, making small talk at holiday parties, thanking her for gift baskets she didn't want. Telling herself she was imagining things, that Richard's late nights and weekend texts were just work, that their marriage was fine because she needed it to be fine.

The plants didn't lie. Maybe that was the appeal.

She was carrying a flat of marigolds toward the herb garden when she stopped. Frank and Marge were by the hoop house, not doing anything remarkable—talking, Frank holding one end of a shade cloth while Marge secured the other. But watching them made Carrie's chest ache. The ease of it. Frank anticipating where Marge needed him without being asked. She said something Carrie couldn't hear, and he laughed—low and warm, like they had all the time in the world.

Forty years. That was what this was. Not performance, not obligation. Partnership.

She and Richard had never looked like that. Not even in the beginning, if she was honest. They'd been good at playing the part—the dinner parties, the vacations, the Christmas cards with everyone smiling. But underneath it, she'd always been reaching for something he wasn't offering. She'd thought that was marriage. She'd thought that was how it worked.

Frank steadied the ladder while Marge climbed down, his hand finding the small of her back as she stepped off—automatic, protective, like he'd done it a thousand times. Carrie realized she'd been settling for so much less than this. For two decades, she'd been settling.

Her phone buzzed in her back pocket.

She almost ignored it. But habit made her pull it out—habit, and the dread that had taken up permanent residence in her stomach.

Gayle Brown, the screen read. Her lawyer.

"Carrie, I'm glad I caught you." Gayle's voice was brisk, professional—the tone she used when delivering news Carrie wouldn't want to hear. "Richard's team sent over a revised settlement offer this morning."

"And?"

"They're claiming the business valuation we submitted is inflated. They've hired their own appraiser, and they're coming in at nearly forty percent lower than our numbers."

Carrie walked toward the far end of the farm, away from where Frank and Marge were still working. "That's not possible. I helped build that company. I know what it's worth."

"I know. And we'll fight it. But Carrie—they're also pushing to accelerate the house sale. Richard's attorney is arguing that maintaining two households is creating undue financial burden on his client." A pause. "They want to force a listing by the end of August."

The end of August. Two months.

The house where she'd raised her daughters. The kitchen where Brittany had learned to bake, where Ava had done homework at the island every afternoon for years. The backyard where they'd had birthday parties and barbecues and one disastrous attempt at a vegetable garden that had produced exactly three tomatoes.

"Can they do that?" Her voice came out steadier than she felt.

"They can try. I'm filing a motion to delay, but I want you to be prepared. If the judge sides with them—"

"I understand."

"We'll talk strategy when you're back. Try to enjoy your vacation."

The line went dead. Carrie stood there, phone in hand, staring at nothing. Five minutes ago the morning had felt like possibility. Now the weight was back, heavier than before.

Behind her, she could hear Marge laughing at something Frank had said. The chickens were making their soft, constant sounds. A breeze moved through the tomato plants, warm and earthy.

She had two months. Maybe less.

When she finally said goodbye—Marge pressing a paper bag of zucchini and early tomatoes into her hands, Frank raising one callused palm in farewell—Carrie's smile felt brittle. They'd invited her back. Told her the job offer stood. But all she could think about was the house, the settlement, the way her life kept narrowing no matter how hard she tried to hold it open.

She drove back toward Sea Isle with the windows down and the radio off, nothing but the sound of tires on pavement and the air rushing past. The gas stations and shopping plazas gave way to beach houses again, the mainland to the causeway, and then the shore rose up ahead of her—narrow and sandy, beautiful and temporary.

The bag of vegetables sat on the passenger seat. Dirt was

embedded under her fingernails, ground into the creases of her palms. Evidence of a morning that had felt, briefly, like possibility.

Gayle said she'd fight it. For now, that would have to be enough.

* * *

Tom was making a charcuterie board.

Not just throwing some cheese on a plate, but actually arranging things—fanning out the salami, clustering the olives, finding the right spot for each cracker. He'd stopped at the gourmet shop in town that afternoon and come back with three kinds of cheese, two salamis, and a jar of honey that cost more than it should have.

Meredith leaned against the counter, watching him work. He'd driven four hours to surprise her, rearranged his whole schedule because he missed her. Because he wanted to be here.

So why did she feel like something was closing in?

"Fig spread or no fig spread?" He held up a small jar.

"Fig spread. Always fig spread."

"That's my girl."

The house had emptied out over the course of the afternoon. The kids were at the pool or the beach or wherever teenagers went when they didn't want to be around adults. The other women had scattered to do their own things.

Just Meredith and Tom in the kitchen, the way it would be in a few months when Sophie was gone and the house was empty and every evening looked like this one.

"I talked to Peterson yesterday," Tom said, arranging crackers in a semicircle. "The numbers work. If he accepts my offer this fall, I could be out by January."

"That fast?"

"Why wait?" He set the board on the island and sat down across from her. "Twenty-two years I've been running that company. Peterson's ready to take over. I'm ready to let him." He spread some brie on a cracker, then added, casually, like it was already decided: "I ran the numbers on your practice too. If you sold, we'd never have to work again. Travel, relax, actually enjoy life for once."

Meredith reached for an olive. Chewed it slowly. Buying time.

"You don't seem excited," he said.

"I'm just thinking."

"About what?"

About the fact that she wasn't ready for this. Tom had already included her in his retirement fantasy—run the numbers, made the plans, assumed she wanted the same exit he did. But she hadn't agreed to anything. She was forty-five. Her mother had worked until sixty-eight. Retirement was for people who were done, and Meredith wasn't done. She loved her job. She was good at it. She'd spent fifteen years building her own practice, her own client list, her own reputation. It was the one thing that was purely hers—separate from Tom, separate from Sophie, separate from this house and these friends and all the roles she played for everyone else.

And what came after? Tom talked about travel and relaxation, vague ideas that sounded nice but didn't add up to a life. What would they actually do all day? Sit across from each other at every meal with nowhere to be?

"It's a lot to process," she said instead. "Big decision."

Tom nodded, accepting this. He didn't push—he never did —and somehow that made it worse. If he'd argued, she could have pushed back. Defined what she was feeling against his resistance. Instead he loved her and trusted her and assumed they wanted the same things.

Did they want the same things?

Twenty-three years. They'd raised a daughter together, built a life together, survived the hard seasons that every marriage faced. They'd argued about money and parenting and whose turn it was to empty the dishwasher, and they'd made up every time because that's what you did when you chose someone.

But she'd also been Meredith-and-Tom for so long she'd forgotten what just-Meredith felt like. And now, right as Sophie was leaving and she might finally have space to figure that out, Tom wanted to retire and be together all the time.

"I was thinking," Tom said, "we could walk over to Sophie's restaurant for dinner. See her in action. Embarrass her a little."

"She'd love that."

"I know. That's why we should do it."

He grinned, and the tension in Meredith's shoulders loosened. This was what she didn't want to lose—this version of them, easy and laughing, before the logistics of retirement turned into another thing to manage.

"Okay," she said. "Let's do it."

They left the house around six-thirty, walking hand in hand down 59th Street toward the restaurant. The evening was still bright, long summer light that stretched the shadows and made everything feel slow and golden. Tom wore a linen shirt he'd packed specifically for dinners out. Meredith wore a sundress she'd bought for this trip, something flowy and floral that she never would have worn at home.

The streets had that early-evening energy—families heading back from the beach, sunburned and tired, a dad pulling a wagon loaded with chairs and umbrellas. A couple walked past with a chocolate lab, and Tom stopped to pet it without asking, the way he always did.

"Remember when Sophie begged us for a dog every summer?" he said, catching up to her.

"She made a PowerPoint presentation. With graphs."

"The responsibility chart. I still think about that chart."

"She would have walked it twice and then it would have been our dog."

"Worth it, though." He fell back into step beside her. "I would have walked that dog every day."

She believed him. That was the thing about Tom—he meant it, every time. He would have walked the dog and done the dishes and shown up, again and again, because that was who he was.

They turned onto Landis Avenue, past shops still crowded with browsers, the restaurants starting to fill. Tom talked about handing over the company, the transition plan, the timeline he was imagining. Retiring didn't mean doing nothing, he said. He had plans. Maybe consulting work, part-time, just enough to stay sharp. Maybe finally learning to surf—a joke, sort of, but also not.

Meredith listened. Asked questions in the right places. Tried to imagine the life he was describing.

"We could travel," Tom said. "Actually travel. Not just long weekends, but real trips. Europe, maybe. That river cruise your mom always talked about."

"My mom wanted to do a river cruise because it meant she didn't have to walk anywhere."

"So we skip the cruise and actually see things. Paris, Rome, Barcelona. Wherever you want."

It sounded nice—everything she'd always said she wanted. And yet.

"I need some time to adjust," Meredith said. "It's not a no. It's—a lot is changing."

"Sophie leaving." Tom nodded. "I know."

The Crabby Catch came into view, its blue awning glowing in the evening light. Through the windows, Meredith could see the dinner crowd starting to fill in—couples at the bar, families at the tables near the front.

Sophie was behind the host podium when they walked in. She looked up from the iPad, saw them, and immediately said, "No."

"We just wanted to say hi," Tom said, all innocence.

"You came to embarrass me. Mom, tell him you came to embarrass me."

"We came to see where you work." Meredith looked around, taking in the nautical décor, the polished wood floors, the bar in the back. "It's nice."

"It's a restaurant. It's exactly what you expected." Sophie's eyes narrowed. "Are you going to sit? Because if you're going to sit, I have to treat you like customers, and that's weird."

"We'll eat at the bar," Meredith said. "We won't even look at you."

"You're looking at me right now."

"After this moment. No more looking."

Sophie rolled her eyes in the theatrical way only a seventeen-year-old could. But there was a grin hiding underneath it, Meredith could tell.

They took seats at the bar, and a woman with short brown hair and reading glasses perched on her head came over with menus. Diane, the manager Sophie had mentioned. She introduced herself briskly, seemed to know exactly who they were, and brought them waters and a bread basket without being asked.

"Your daughter's a natural," Diane said. "First week and she's already handling the rush better than kids who've been here since May."

"She's always been organized," Tom said. "Gets it from her mother."

Meredith caught Sophie glancing over from the host podium, checking to make sure they weren't causing a scene. An older couple walked in—pink-shouldered, in no rush—and Sophie greeted them, grabbed menus, led them to a corner booth with an ocean view.

Ethan came out of the kitchen, carrying a plastic bin of dishes. He looked different than he had at the house—more focused, more present, the perpetual scowl replaced with concentration. He moved between tables efficiently, clearing plates, wiping surfaces, stacking things like someone who'd already learned the routine.

"Ethan's working here too?" Tom asked.

"He just started. Same time as Sophie."

"Good for him." Tom watched Ethan work for a moment. "He seems like he's got a lot going on."

"His dad's getting remarried. To someone not much older than Sophie."

Tom whistled low. "That'll do it."

A server came through from the patio—college-aged, relaxed, tan in a way that suggested he'd grown up spending summers here. He stopped at the host podium, leaning against it to say something to Sophie. She laughed—really laughed, not the polite version Meredith knew so well—and then she reached up and touched his arm. Brief, almost nothing. Her fingertips against his forearm, a gesture so small it might have meant nothing.

Except Meredith saw Sophie's whole posture change. How she angled toward him, her smile softer than it had been a moment ago. The server—Jake, she'd heard Diane call him— looked at Sophie like she'd said something brilliant instead of whatever small joke had passed between them.

Sophie's phone buzzed on the podium. She glanced at it, and Meredith watched her daughter's face shift—the softness disappearing, replaced by an expression more careful. More composed. She typed a quick reply without picking it up.

Trevor. It had to be Trevor.

And the way Sophie had glanced at her phone was nothing like how she'd looked at Jake.

Meredith's stomach dropped.

"Don't," Tom said quietly.

"Don't what?"

"Whatever you're thinking. Don't."

"I wasn't thinking anything."

"You were thinking about getting involved. About warning

her, or guiding her, or whatever it is you do when you think one of your people is about to make a mistake." Tom set down his glass. "She's seventeen. Let her make her own choices."

"Even if they're bad ones?"

"Especially then." He met her eyes. "She'll figure it out."

Meredith looked at her daughter across the restaurant. Sophie was helping another family now, menus in hand, smile professional but genuine. She handled the job like she handled everything—competently, carefully, with just enough personality to make people like her.

She was going to be fine. College in the fall, a whole future ahead of her, a life that would take her further and further from the girl who'd built sandcastles on this beach and cried over jellyfish stings.

But Trevor was at home, waiting. Texting. Planning for a future Sophie might already be drifting away from.

"I'm not ready," Meredith said. She meant Sophie leaving. She meant all of it.

Tom reached over and took her hand. "Nobody is. That's not the point."

They finished dinner and left cash on the bar. Sophie waved to them on the way out—a real wave, not the dismissive flick she'd given when they arrived. Ethan nodded from across the room, barely looking up from his work.

At the door, Meredith glanced back one more time. Jake had returned to the patio, but Sophie was watching him go—a second, maybe two, long enough for Meredith to catch it before her daughter refocused on the podium and her phone and the text she still hadn't answered.

CHAPTER SIX

Driftwood Coffee was quiet, the lull between the early rush and the lunch crowd.

Jen ordered at the counter and scanned the room while she waited. Corner tables, a couple with a stroller near the door, two women deep in conversation over what looked like the day's plans. The table by the window was open.

Coffee in hand, she claimed the window table and opened her laptop before she could talk herself out of it. The document labeled "DON'T DELETE" was right where she'd left it, cursor blinking after the last sentence she'd written. More pages now than when she'd started. She'd been adding to it in stolen hours, early mornings, late nights when the house was quiet.

It was ridiculous. It was nothing like what she was supposed to be writing. Her editor was waiting for the next Clementine Fields. The series that had built her career, paid off her mortgage, given her the life she'd carefully constructed over fifteen years of deadlines.

She scrolled through the fantasy pages instead.

The prose was looser here, less careful. She'd stopped thinking about word counts and chapter breaks and whether the red herrings were planted early enough. She'd written. And for three days, that had been enough.

A shadow passed the window, and then he was there—pushing through the door, bag over one shoulder, already scanning for an open table.

Same guy from last time. Same spaceship paperback, same restless energy. He ordered at the counter, waited for his coffee, then claimed the corner table and set up: laptop open, book beside his cup.

Then he looked up and caught her looking.

She looked away first. Pulled up the cozy mystery file, seventy-five percent done and stalled for months, and pretended to read the last paragraph.

Clementine set her teacup down with more force than necessary. "Mr. Ashworth, I don't care how many alibis you claim to have. Someone moved that grandfather clock, and I intend to find out why."

She'd written that sentence months ago—the start of the final act—and hadn't been able to find the next one since.

She stared at the screen. The fantasy romance waited in the other tab, alive and demanding in ways the mystery hadn't been in a long time.

"Outlet situation in the corner is terrible," a voice said.

Her eyes lifted from the screen. He was standing beside her table, laptop tucked under one arm, coffee in the other hand. Up close, she saw details she'd missed before. The silver ring on his thumb, the faded venue name on his T-shirt now close enough to almost read. A date from years ago.

"There's one under the window," she said, gesturing. "You have to move the chair."

"Ah." He crouched down, found it, and straightened with a satisfied nod. "Crisis averted." He didn't move to leave. "I noticed you're here again."

The outlet had been a pretense. She didn't mind.

"I noticed you noticing."

He laughed, surprised out of himself. "Fair enough." He set his coffee on the table and extended his hand. "Clint."

"Jen."

He accepted that with a nod, which she appreciated. "Mind if I join you? Seems a shame to waste a working outlet."

She was here to work. She had a mystery to write, an editor to appease, a career to maintain.

"Go ahead," she said, and moved her bag off the chair across from her.

They worked in parallel for the first hour. Not silence, really. There was the ambient noise of the coffee shop, the whir of the espresso machine, someone's phone buzzing every few minutes. But they didn't talk. Clint had one earbud in, the other dangling loose. He worked the way he had last time. Bursts of typing, phone checks, the paperback for resets. She matched his rhythm, typing when he typed, pausing when he paused.

Once, she glanced up to rest her eyes and found him watching her over the top of his laptop. He looked back at his screen without saying anything, but she'd caught it.

At some point, she noticed two full pages on the screen. Not the mystery. The fantasy. The world with two moons had pulled her back in, and she'd stopped fighting it.

"Can I ask you something?"

Her attention lifted. Clint had pushed his laptop aside, focused entirely on her.

"Depends on the question."

"What are you working on? You've got that look."

"What look?"

"The one where you're somewhere else entirely. Like whatever's on that screen has you completely absorbed." He smiled, sheepish. "I only ask because I haven't had that look in about six months, and I'm trying to figure out how to get it back."

She could have said "just work stuff" and left it there. But the question felt honest, the admission embedded inside it, and she told him the truth.

"I'm supposed to be writing a cozy mystery. It's what I do. What I've always done." She gestured at the screen, then dropped her hand. "But for the last few months, this other thing has been happening instead. Fantasy romance. A woman at the edge of a forest that shouldn't exist, magic she doesn't understand yet." She heard herself and winced. "It sounds ridiculous when I say it out loud."

"It doesn't sound ridiculous." Clint leaned forward, elbows on the table. "It sounds like the thing that actually wants to exist."

"That's not how publishing works."

"No. But it's how making things works." He picked up his coffee, found it empty, set it back down. "I play guitar in a band. We've been together almost twelve years. We tour most of the year, put out a record every couple of years. Nothing you'd hear on the radio, but we've built something real. Enough of a following that this is all I do." No false modesty in it. "We're doing a summer residency at the Hard Rock in Atlantic City this year. Thursdays through August."

That explained the calluses on his fingertips.

"That sounds amazing."

"It is. It was." He ran a hand through his hair. "But lately I've been writing stuff that doesn't fit what we do. Different sound, different feel. The guys aren't sure about it." He shrugged. "So I started slipping one or two into the sets anyway. To see what happens."

"So what do you do?"

"Come here. Stare at the screen. Read someone else's book and feel jealous of how easily it seems to have come to them." He gestured at the paperback. "Same as everyone else."

"That's bleak."

"Little bit." But he was smiling. "What's the fantasy about? If you don't mind me asking."

She explained it. The hero who appeared from the tree line like he'd been waiting for her. The slow burn between them as he taught her to see the magic. The secrets he was keeping, and the ones she didn't know she had. Clint asked questions, good ones, the kind that made her think harder about things she'd written instinctively. He didn't laugh. He didn't tell her it sounded like every other fantasy romance on the market.

Somewhere in the middle of explaining, she realized he wasn't just listening. His eyes were on her face, following the way her hands moved when she talked. She lost her train of thought for a second then found it again.

By the time she finished, something in Jen had loosened. Not because he'd given her answers, but because he'd listened like what she was making mattered, even the messy, unfinished, not-supposed-to-exist version of it.

"You already know what you want to do," Clint said. "You're just afraid of what happens if you actually do it."

"It's not that simple."

"It's exactly that simple." He held her gaze. "It's just not easy."

She was about to respond when a voice cut through the coffee shop noise.

"Oh my gosh. Oh my gosh, oh my gosh."

A woman had stopped beside their table. Midfifties, vacation tan, oversized sunglasses pushed up into blond hair. She was staring at Jen with the intensity of someone who had just recognized a celebrity.

"You're Amber Carr, aren't you? I knew it. I said to my husband, I said, that woman at the coffee shop looks just like Amber Carr, and he said I was being ridiculous, but I'm never wrong about these things."

Her face warmed. Surprise, a flush of pride she hadn't expected. She'd been nobody for an hour. Now she was Amber Carr again.

"I've read every single Clementine Fields mystery," the

woman continued, not waiting for confirmation. "Every single one. I started with *A Bitter Brew in Brambleton* and I've been hooked ever since. My book club did *Murder at the May Ball* last spring, and half of us thought the gardener did it, but I knew it was the professor's wife. Something about the way she kept bringing up the orchids."

Across the table, Clint was listening to all of this. Jen kept her eyes on the woman.

"Thank you," Jen said. "That really means a lot. The orchid detail, I worked so hard on that clue, hoping someone would catch it. You have a good eye."

"And the new one, when is the new one coming out? We've been waiting ages. Clementine and Detective Stovers, are they finally going to get together? My friend Linda says there's too much romantic tension to keep them apart much longer, and I have to agree."

"I'm still working on it," Jen said, managing a real smile. "But I promise it'll be worth the wait. And thank you. Readers like you are the reason I get to keep doing this."

"Well, don't keep us waiting too long." The woman reached into her purse and pulled out a receipt and a pen. "Could I get an autograph? For my friend Linda. She's going to die when she finds out I met you."

Jen signed the receipt. Smiled for the photo the woman insisted on taking. She told the woman how much it meant to meet readers like her, how book clubs were her favorite audiences, and promised Linda would get her answers soon.

When the woman left at last—still talking, waving the signed receipt like a trophy—the ease between them had shifted.

"Amber Carr," Clint said quietly. He wasn't looking at her like she was famous. He was rethinking her. "That's a big deal."

"Most days it doesn't feel like that." She tried for lightness. "Most days it feels like deadlines."

"And today?"

She thought about it. "Today it felt good."

He nodded slowly then smiled. "So you're the one with the real deadline pressure. And here I am complaining about my band."

"Yours counts too," she said.

"I'm glad I came over," he said. No irony in it.

Before she could figure out how to respond, his phone buzzed on the table. He glanced at it then grimaced. "Band stuff. We're supposed to run through the new material before Thursday." He started gathering his things. Laptop, bag, the paperback. "I'm sorry, I have to run."

"No, of course. Go."

He stood, then paused. Let his eyes hold hers. "We play Thursdays at the Hard Rock. Nine o'clock." Not quite an invitation. Just information. "In case you want to hear what I've been working on."

"Maybe," she said.

"I hope so." He smiled, quick but guarded, and headed for the door.

The coffee shop went back to its background hum.

Jen sat alone at the table, eyes on the empty chair across from her. The conversation had ended too soon. Interrupted by a fan, then a phone call, then the regular demands of a Thursday. But he'd invited her to see him play. And he'd been sincere when he said he was glad he came over. She'd seen it in his face.

The Hard Rock. Thursdays. Atlantic City.

She opened her email. Amanda's latest was a week old now. *Marketing needs fifty pages by end of month. Even rough is fine. Let me know how it's going?*

Two weeks. She had two hundred pages. What she didn't have was an ending.

Jen had been telling Amanda for months that she was almost done. Tightening the final act, she'd said. Just landing the reveal. All of it stalling. The longer she waited, the harder it got to admit she was stuck. The fantasy romance had been a distraction at first, a way to keep the words flowing while she figured out how to finish Clementine. But now the distraction had become the thing she actually wanted to write.

Readers like you are the reason I get to keep doing this.

Those words had surprised her. Under the deadline panic and the block and the guilt, she still believed them. That woman, Linda's friend, had been hooked since *A Bitter Brew in Brambleton*. Had argued about suspects with her book club. Had waited, genuinely waited, to find out if Clementine and Detective Stovers would figure it out.

Those readers deserved an ending.

Jen opened the cozy mystery file. Scrolled past the two hundred pages that worked, down to the place where she'd stopped. The cursor waited after that last line, patient as ever.

She put her fingers on the keys. To see.

The grandfather clock had been moved six inches to the left. Clementine measured it twice to be certain, ignoring the way Detective Stovers watched her from the doorway with that infuriating half-smile. She was close now. She could feel it.

She read it back. It wasn't terrible.

She kept typing.

* * *

The parking lot at Cape May Point State Park was nearly full by early afternoon.

Olivia found a spot near the trailhead and sat for a moment, watching families unload from minivans and couples lace up hiking shoes. Beyond the lot, trails wound through woods and wetlands toward the beach. Quieter than Sea Isle, no promenade crowds, no shops or restaurants. Just the rustle of wind through the trees and birdsong from somewhere deeper in the woods.

Michael was already there, leaning against the wooden

railing at the trailhead. He pushed off when he saw her car pull in, then seemed to catch himself, force himself to wait.

She got out. Grabbed her water bottle. Walked toward him with a steadiness she didn't feel.

This was the first time she'd seen him since their carpool days back home. The hiking group, the coffee runs afterward. It had all felt innocent then. Just two people who enjoyed the same trails, the same easy silences that came from walking through woods together.

But then February happened. Dan's phone on the kitchen counter. Rachel's name lighting up the screen. After that, the texts with Michael felt like something else entirely.

"Hey." He straightened as she approached. Up close, he was as she remembered. Not classically handsome, but interesting. Brown eyes that paid attention. A slight crookedness to his nose, like it had been broken once and set imperfectly.

"Hey yourself."

"Ready?"

"Always."

They started down the boardwalk, side by side, the wooden planks stretching ahead through the trees. The canopy filtered the sunlight into shifting patterns around them, and the air was cool and damp. Leaves and earth, a trace of honeysuckle. Shaded and still.

"I forgot how much I needed this," Olivia said. "Trees. Actual trees."

"The beach is nice, but it's a lot of... exposure." Michael ducked under a low branch. "Sometimes you want walls. Even if they're made of leaves."

They walked. The trail wound deeper into the woods, the sounds of the parking lot fading behind them. At one point, Michael stopped and pointed. A black snake sunning itself on a flat rock just off the path.

"Don't move," he said, though she hadn't been about to.

They watched it together. The snake seemed unbothered,

soaking up the warmth, utterly still except for the occasional flick of its tongue.

"Beautiful," Olivia said quietly.

"Most people would run."

"Their loss."

The snake slid off the rock and disappeared into the underbrush. They kept walking.

Michael noticed things. That was part of what she'd always liked about him. A hawk circling overhead. A cluster of wildflowers she would have walked right past. He asked questions about her work, the art history stuff, and remembered the answers. Remembered details from conversations they'd had months ago.

"How's the research going?" he asked. "The Eakins project?"

She blinked. She'd mentioned the Eakins project exactly once, during a car ride back in March. "Still gathering sources. The archive access has been complicated."

"But you got the grant, right? The one you were waiting on?"

"I did. Last month." She hadn't told Dan about the grant. He hadn't asked.

They walked on. The conversation moved easily. Books they'd read, places they wanted to travel, the frustrations of academic bureaucracy. Nothing that would have looked wrong from the outside. Two colleagues, two friends, enjoying a walk through nature.

But Olivia felt it underneath. The awareness of where he was in space, how close his arm was to hers as they walked. Her pulse quickening when he held her gaze a moment too long.

The trail opened up as they reached the lakes at the end. The trees fell away, and there was sky again—wide and blue, the lighthouse visible in the distance. A pair of swans drifted on the nearer lake, their reflections perfect on the still surface.

Beyond them, the second lake glinted in the sun, an egret standing motionless at its edge.

Michael stopped. "This is the spot."

"It really is."

They stood there, taking it in. The quiet was different here. The hush of the woods replaced by the sound of waves beyond the dunes.

"Olivia, I need to tell you something."

She went still. "Okay."

"I'm not just down for the weekend." He was looking at her now, fully, the way he did when he was about to say something he'd been thinking about for a while. "I rented a place. In Avalon. For the summer."

She didn't say anything. The summer had just gotten more complicated.

"I know how that sounds. I know it's—" He rubbed the back of his neck. "A friend had a share in Avalon. He bailed last minute, needed someone to take it. I said yes because I needed to get away." He paused. "Then I remembered you'd be in Sea Isle. Fifteen minutes away. I wanted you to know."

The swans drifted closer together on the water. The egret hadn't moved. Everything as it had been sixty seconds ago, and nothing the same.

"I'm not asking for anything. I know things are complicated for you." He held up his hands, palms out. "I just wanted to be honest about it. I'm here. You're here. That's all."

Her heart was beating too fast.

They stood there, the confession suspended between them. On the lake, one of the swans dipped its head beneath the surface and came up again, water streaming from its neck.

"We should head back," Olivia said at last.

They did. But the silence was different now, heavy with what he'd said, with what she hadn't.

At one point, the trail dipped down through a stretch of soft sand between the dunes. Olivia's foot caught on a buried root, and Michael's hand shot out, catching her elbow, steadying her.

"Careful."

His hand lingered. She felt the pressure of each finger through the thin fabric of her shirt.

"Thanks," she said, and he let go.

Neither of them acknowledged it. But when they started walking again, she was aware of every inch of space between them. How easily it could change.

The trail curved back toward the parking lot, dunes rising to their left, another pond glinting through the reeds. They passed families with binoculars, a couple holding hands, a woman jogging with earbuds in. Normal people doing normal things on a normal summer day.

Olivia wondered what they saw when they looked at her. A woman walking with a man who wasn't her husband. Nothing unusual. Nothing scandalous. A pair of hikers sharing the path.

Except she knew better.

"I'm not going to push," Michael said, as the parking lot came into view. "Whatever you decide, I'll respect it. But I'll be here. If you want to talk. Or walk. Or anything."

She nodded. She didn't know what to say.

They reached the lot. He walked her to her car, not touching, not even close enough to suggest it. Present. Waiting.

"I need time," she said.

"I know."

"I don't know what I'm doing."

"Neither do I." He smiled, barely. "But you know where to find me."

She got in the car and started the engine.

He stood there as she backed out of the space, still watching as she turned for the exit. In her rearview mirror, she saw him finally move, walking to his own car with his hands in his pockets.

The drive back to Sea Isle took thirty minutes. Olivia's hands shook on the wheel the entire way.

He'd come here for his own reasons. But he'd reached out to her. Told her what he wanted and left the decision in her lap.

And the terrifying part—the part that made her grip tighten on the wheel—was that she wasn't as guilty as she should be.

She was thrilled.

She tried to remember the walk, what they'd talked about, whether she'd given him any indication. But the details blurred, overwhelmed by the single sharp memory of his hand on her elbow.

On the Parkway, heading north, she realized something else. For two hours on that trail, she hadn't thought about Dan. Hadn't thought about the twins, the house, the marriage she was supposed to be saving.

That shook her too. Not just what Michael had said, but that she'd let herself forget her actual life so completely.

She pulled into the driveway at the rental house and sat there, engine off.

Dan's text from this morning was still unanswered. *Miss you. Hope the hike was nice. Call me when you get a chance?*

She should call him. She should tell him she loved him, that she missed him too, that they were going to figure this out together.

But her mind kept returning to the trail. The pressure of his fingers through her sleeve. His voice when he'd said *I'm here. You're here.* Like it was the truest thing he'd ever admitted.

Inside the house, she could hear voices. Lily and Max arguing about something, Meredith calling from the kitchen, the familiar sounds of a vacation in progress.

She had to go in. She had to act like nothing had changed.

But she sat in the car another minute, watching the afternoon light shift across the dashboard, waiting for her breath to steady.

The dinner rush had finally broken.

Sophie wiped down menus at the hostess stand, her feet throbbing in the black flats she'd bought specifically for this job. The birthday party from the patio had left after two hours and three requests to speak to a manager. The couple who'd sent back their crab cakes had eventually found something they liked. Diane had nodded at her on the way to the back office. From Diane, that counted.

Through the front windows, the sky had gone that deep blue that came just before the streetlights kicked on.

She was stacking menus when Ethan came in from outside, bus tub balanced on his hip. He looked tired but focused, head down, getting it done.

"Hey," Sophie said.

"Hey." He paused long enough to shift the tub's weight. "Diane's looking for you. Maria called out, and she needs someone to help break down the patio."

"Got it. Thanks."

He nodded and kept moving toward the kitchen. They'd grown up together, more or less—beach weeks and holidays and the occasional birthday party when their moms coordinated. Not quite siblings, but close. The kind of close where you didn't have to talk unless something was actually happening.

Sophie found Diane in the back office. When she got to the patio, Jake was pulling tablecloths and draping them over the railing. He looked up when she stepped outside, and something in his expression changed—not the easy grin he used with customers. Less guarded. He'd changed shirts since the dinner rush—this one was softer, gray instead of black. She shouldn't have noticed that.

"Heard you got drafted," he said.

"I don't mind. The house is full of adults drinking wine on the deck, and I didn't feel like answering questions about my first week."

The patio was scattered with the debris of dinner service—tea lights burned to stubs, napkins that had blown off tables, a kid's crayon abandoned under a chair. Sophie collected candle holders while Jake worked through the tables. Her eyes kept drifting to his hands as he folded—quick, confident movements. She made herself look away.

"Question for you," Jake said without looking up.

"Depends."

"Why'd you take this job? You're here for the summer, right? Most people just want to be on the beach."

Sophie set a handful of candle holders on the nearest table. She'd asked herself the same thing during the worst of the rush.

"I needed something separate," she said. "Everyone in that house has their own stuff going on. My mom, her friends. And I just—" She wasn't sure how to finish.

"Wanted to be somewhere they weren't watching?"

"Yeah."

Jake wasn't like the tourist kids who came through—the ones whose parents belonged to the beach club, who treated Sea Isle like a photo opportunity. He belonged here.

Once, between tasks, his eyes drifted to her instead of the linen in his hands. When she glanced over, he went back to folding.

"My boyfriend thinks it's weird," she said. "That I wanted to work. He keeps asking why I don't just relax."

Something crossed Jake's face when she said "boyfriend." Quick, then gone.

"What do you tell him?"

"That I like staying busy." She kept clearing. "But that's not really it."

Jake stopped working.

"He has everything figured out," Sophie said. "Where he's applying to college, what he wants to study, his whole five-year plan. He knows exactly who he's going to be. And I don't. I don't know any of it. But I can't say that to him because he'll want to fix it. Make a plan."

"Some things don't need plans."

"Try telling him that."

They finished the patio without talking. Sophie had opened up more than she'd planned, and Jake hadn't tried to fix any of it.

Inside, Diane was locking up the register. "You two good to finish? I've got to drop my daughter off at a sleepover—I'm already late."

"We've got it," Jake said.

Diane took her keys and left. Sophie found the broom in the supply closet and started sweeping near the hostess stand.

"For what it's worth," Jake said, wiping down the bar, "he sounds exhausting."

Sophie laughed. "He's not. He's just... certain."

"Same thing sometimes."

Her phone buzzed in her apron. She ignored it.

It buzzed again. And again.

She pulled it out. Three texts from Trevor.

Hey, so I've been thinking

What if I came down for a weekend? Maybe Fourth of July?

I miss you and it would be fun to see the beach house

Two weeks ago, she would have been excited. Trevor here, meeting her mom's friends, seeing where she worked, walking the promenade after her shifts.

Now the thought made her uneasy.

"Everything okay?" Jake had paused, rag in hand.

"Yeah. My boyfriend wants to visit."

"That's good, right?"

"Right," she said. "That's good."

She went back to sweeping. Trevor in Sea Isle. Trevor meeting everyone. Trevor asking about her coworkers in that friendly way he had, expecting her to be excited to tell him.

They finished closing in another twenty minutes. Jake walked her out the back. The air smelled like fryer grease and salt, and music spilled out of a bar up the street.

"See you tomorrow?" Jake said.

"Four to close."

"Same." He headed toward wherever he'd parked, keys already in his hand.

Sophie walked home along the promenade instead of cutting through the side streets. Trevor's texts sat unanswered in her phone.

He wanted to see her. Wanted to spend a holiday weekend with her, meet the people in her summer, be part of it.

She should text him back. She didn't.

CHAPTER SEVEN

Brittany had been at the beach club for almost a week now, long enough to know how it all worked.

Mornings started slow. Members trickling in, claiming their usual spots, ordering the same drinks they'd ordered every day since June began. The lunch rush hit around noon and lasted until two. Then the lull, when the families with young kids packed up and the serious tanners settled in for the afternoon, and the pool deck went quiet except for the splash of someone diving in and the low murmur of conversation.

She'd gotten the hang of it. The rhythms of the desk, the names of the regulars, the smile that came automatically now when someone approached. The beach club paid well and tipped better, and most of the members were fine. Some were even nice. The ones who remembered her name, who asked how her summer was going, who said please and thank you without making it sound like a chore.

And then there were the others.

Mrs. Campbell arrived at eleven-thirty, which was earlier than usual. Brittany saw her coming from across the deck. Designer sunglasses, oversized hat, the stride of someone who expected the path to clear itself.

"Good morning," Brittany said as she approached. "How can I help you?"

"My cabana." Mrs. Campbell removed her sunglasses. "It's occupied."

Brittany checked the tablet. "I have you down for Cabana 4, starting at noon."

"I reserved it for eleven."

"The system shows noon. Let me just—"

"I specifically requested eleven. I spoke with someone on the phone yesterday. Whoever it was clearly made an error." She sighed loudly, glancing around like she was looking for anyone more competent. "Is this your first week?"

"I've been here almost a week, yes, but—"

"That explains it."

Brittany scanned the notes. Nothing about an eleven o'clock request. Cabana 4 had been booked from ten to twelve by another member, the Hardings, who were currently using it, their children's sand toys scattered across the deck.

"I apologize for the mix-up," Brittany said, keeping her voice even. "It looks like there may have been a miscommunication. Cabana 4 is currently in use, but it should be available at noon as scheduled. Can I offer you a chair on the deck while you wait, or perhaps—"

"I don't want a chair on the deck." Mrs. Campbell's voice had risen. People were looking. "I want my cabana. The one I reserved. At eleven. This is ridiculous."

"I understand, and I'm sorry for the inconvenience. Unfortunately, the Hardings have the cabana until noon. I can check if any other cabanas are available—"

"I don't want another cabana. I want Cabana 4. It's the only one with adequate shade at this hour, which is why I specifically requested it for eleven." She looked Brittany up and down. "I need to speak with someone who can actually help me."

The Harding children were staring now. So was the couple

at the bar. So was Ryan, who'd paused mid-pour to watch the exchange.

Brittany felt the heat rising to her face. "Let me get the manager—"

"Yes. Do that."

The manager appeared before Brittany could move. It was Pam, who'd been hovering near the pool and had probably heard the whole thing. She cut across the deck without hurrying, the way someone moves when they've done this before.

"Mrs. Campbell, always lovely to see you. What seems to be the issue?"

Mrs. Campbell repeated her complaint, this time with additional details about her phone call, her specific requests, her long-standing membership, her expectations of service. Pam nodded along, making sympathetic sounds, occasionally glancing at Brittany with an expression that was impossible to read.

"I completely understand," Pam said when she'd finished. "This is clearly our mistake, and I'm so sorry for the confusion. Brittany, could you ask the Hardings if they'd be willing to relocate to Cabana 7? It has excellent afternoon shade, and we can offer them complimentary drinks for the inconvenience."

Brittany stared at her. The Hardings had done nothing wrong. They'd booked their cabana through the proper channels and arrived on time. And now she was supposed to ask them to move because someone else had thrown a fit?

"Of course," she said, because what else could she say?

She walked to Cabana 4. Mrs. Harding looked up from her magazine, already resigned.

"I'm so sorry," Brittany said quietly. "There's been a scheduling error with the reservations. Would you mind relocating to Cabana 7? We'll comp your drinks for the afternoon."

Mrs. Harding glanced toward the desk, where Mrs. Campbell was gathering her things with an air of vindication. Then she turned back to Brittany.

"It's fine," she said, though it clearly wasn't. "Kids, pack up. We're moving."

The Harding children complained. Mrs. Harding shushed them. Brittany helped carry the sand toys to the new cabana, face burning, stomach in a knot.

When she returned to the front desk, Pam pulled her aside. "A word?"

They stepped into the small office behind the check-in area. Pam closed the door.

"You handled that well," she said, "but I need you to be more proactive about managing expectations. When a member says they made a specific request, we accommodate. Even if the system doesn't reflect it."

"But the system—"

"The system isn't the point. Member satisfaction is the point." Pam's voice dropped. "Mrs. Campbell is on the board. Her husband's family has been members here for thirty years. It's not about who's right. It's about who's here."

Brittany nodded. Said the things she was supposed to say. Left the office feeling like she'd swallowed something sharp.

The deck had gone back to normal. Mrs. Campbell had installed herself in Cabana 4, drink in hand, triumphant. The Hardings were in Cabana 7, their children splashing in the shallow end of the pool.

Brittany returned to her station. Pulled up the tablet. Checked in the next member with a brightness she didn't feel.

At three o'clock, she took her break.

The staff break area was a small patio behind the main building, hidden from member view by a hedge and a fence. A few plastic chairs, a table with an ashtray nobody used anymore, a view of the service entrance and the dumpsters.

Brittany sat down and put her head in her hands.

"Rough day?"

She looked up. Ryan had appeared with two glasses of

water, condensation beading on the sides. He handed her one and dropped into the chair across from her.

"You could say that."

"The Campbell thing?" He shook his head. "I watched the whole exchange. You were way more professional than she deserved."

"Didn't help much."

"It never does." He leaned back in his chair, stretching his legs out.

"How do you deal with it?" Brittany asked, turning the glass in her hands.

"Remind myself it's temporary. They don't actually know me, so what they think doesn't mean anything." He took a sip of water. "And I focus on what I'm working toward. What this is all leading to."

"What's that?"

"College. Environmental engineering, maybe. Something that keeps me near the water but isn't about serving drinks to people who don't see me."

Brittany looked at him differently then. She'd assumed he was just another summer worker, putting in hours, killing time. She was revising that.

"That sounds like a real plan."

"More like a goal. We'll see if I get there." He shrugged. "You?"

"I don't have one yet. I'm a college sophomore. Everyone keeps asking what I want to do with my life like I'm supposed to have an answer."

"You don't need an answer yet. Just keep asking the question."

They sat together in silence for a minute. The hedge rustled in the breeze. A radio played from inside, nineties rock, a song her parents would know.

"There's a thing tonight," Ryan said. "Some people from

work, some locals. Bonfire down by the jetty. Nothing fancy, just hanging out."

Brittany studied him. "A bonfire?"

"It's kind of a tradition. Every couple of weeks, when the weather's good. The summer people have their deck parties. We have this."

"And you're inviting me."

"You work here. That makes you one of us." He finished his water. "Come if you want. Don't come if you don't. No pressure."

He stood, collected both glasses, and headed back toward the bar.

Brittany stayed on the patio for another few minutes, watching the hedge sway.

* * *

The bonfire was down past the jetty, south of the main beach, in a stretch of sand that belonged to no particular street or address.

Brittany had told the moms she was meeting some people from work. The moms hadn't pried. Sophie had given her a look—she'd already drawn her own conclusions—and Brittany had ignored it.

She walked down the beach as the light faded, sneakers in hand, the sand still holding the day's heat. The town was settling into evening behind her, the boardwalk thinning out, the restaurants winding down from dinner, families heading home to shower off the salt and sun.

The bonfire glowed ahead, throwing shadows onto the jetty rocks.

They were spread out on blankets and towels, maybe fifteen people, maybe more. Someone had a cooler. Someone else had a speaker playing something mellow, acoustic guitar and a voice that blurred with the crash of the waves. A few faces she recognized from the club. Most she didn't.

Ryan was already on his feet, walking toward her. He moved loose and easy, like he had nowhere else to be, and it caught her off guard.

"You made it." He stopped in front of her, looking genuinely pleased.

"I almost talked myself out of it three times on the walk over."

"But you didn't."

"But I didn't."

He smiled. The fire caught his face at an angle, and she noticed his eyes were more gray than blue.

He led her to the group, introducing her to names she knew she wouldn't remember. Jess, who worked at the surf shop. Miguel, who was a lifeguard on the north beach. A girl named Dana who apparently bartended at a place on Landis and had been doing this bonfire thing since high school.

"First summer down?" Dana asked.

"First summer working," Brittany said. "I've been coming to Sea Isle my whole life."

"Different when you're behind the desk," Dana said.

"Very different."

They made room for her on a blanket near the fire. Someone passed her a beer, and she took it. The waves rolled in steady and regular, catching the last light before darkness settled completely.

"So." Dana stretched out on the sand, propping herself on her elbows. "Beach club. That's rough."

"It's not that bad."

"You're a better liar than I was my first year."

Brittany laughed. "Okay. It's pretty bad."

"The members are the worst. Some of them, anyway. They forget that we're people."

"There was a woman today—" She trailed off. But they

were all looking at her, and the fire and the beer and how quickly everyone had welcomed her in, and she started talking. The cabana came out. The demand. Pam's quiet talk in the office.

"Campbell?" Miguel said. "I worked the club last summer. She's legendary. Got a bartender fired for putting one too many ice cubes in her gin and tonic."

"One ice cube?"

"She has a system."

"That's insane," Brittany said.

"That's the club." Dana picked at the label on her bottle. "You learn who to avoid. You learn who tips well and who complains no matter what. It's a game. Play it right and you make decent money. Play it wrong and you're doing double shifts until Labor Day."

The conversation shifted. Other stories, other members, a mythology of the beach club that Brittany was only beginning to understand. She listened more than she talked, nursing her beer, letting the fire heat her face while her back stayed cool.

At some point, the group broke apart. People wandered to other blankets, other conversations. The music changed to something with a little more bass. Another log landed on the fire.

Ryan dropped onto the blanket next to her.

"Thanks," she said. "For inviting me."

"Sure." He stretched out, propping himself on one elbow. "Having fun?"

"More than I expected." She watched the sparks drift upward. "Today was rough."

"The Campbell thing?"

She nodded.

"You fit fine here." He bumped his shoulder against hers. "Better than fine."

She didn't pull away.

The fire had burned lower. People were still talking in clusters, but the energy had shifted, quieter now, more intimate. The waves were louder than the music, and the stars had come out thick and bright in a way they never did back home.

"Can I ask you something?" Brittany said.

"Go for it."

"You mentioned environmental engineering earlier. Is that really what you want?"

Ryan stretched out on the blanket, hands behind his head. "Most people think I'm kidding when I say stuff like that. Like I'm just some guy who works at a beach club."

"I didn't think you were kidding."

He turned his head to look at her. In the firelight, he was all angles and shadows.

"My grandfather used to take me crabbing out on the bay when I was a kid," he said. "Same spots his dad took him. Except half of them don't work anymore. The water's different. The grass beds are disappearing. Last summer we couldn't find blue crabs where they'd always been." He paused. "That's not supposed to happen in one generation."

"That's sad."

"It's motivating." He sat up, wrapping his arms around his knees. "I want to understand what's causing it and figure out how to fix it. Water quality, runoff, all the stuff that's changing the ecosystem. That's what environmental engineers do."

She studied his face. Not the side of him she'd assumed, the ease, the confidence. This was different.

"That's not what I expected you to say."

"What did you expect?"

"Something lighter, maybe. Party stories. Beach stuff."

"I like beach stuff." He grinned. "I just like knowing it'll still be here in fifty years."

The fire popped. A scatter of sparks rose into the air and vanished.

"What about you?" Ryan asked. "What do you want?"

"I'm not sure yet." She picked at the edge of the blanket.

"I'm supposed to be figuring out my major, my career, my life. Everyone acts like I should have a plan by now."

"I probably made it sound like I have mine together." He looked out at the water. "I don't. I just found one thing I care about. Everything else is still a question mark."

"That's more than I have."

"It's one thing, Brittany. One." He turned back to her. "I don't know where I'll get in, or if I can afford it, or if I'll be any good at it. I just know I want to try."

She didn't say anything for a moment. The honesty surprised her.

"That helps, actually," she said. "Everyone else makes it sound like they've got the whole map."

"Nobody has the map. Some people are just better at pretending."

"That sounds like something from a self-help book."

"My mom reads a lot of self-help books. Apparently some of it stuck."

She laughed. The tension she'd been carrying all day, the cabana, the talking-to, felt further away now.

Someone called Ryan's name from the other side of the fire. He ignored it.

"We should probably rejoin the group," Brittany said.

"Probably."

They stayed where they were.

The fire crackled. The waves kept rolling in. Somewhere down the beach, someone laughed loud enough to carry over the water.

"Tonight was better with you here," Ryan said, his voice lower now.

"Yeah." She smiled. "It was."

A pause.

Then Dana's voice cut through—"Ryan, get over here, we need you for this debate"—and the moment slipped past.

He got to his feet, brushing sand from his shorts. Offered

her a hand up. She took it, and for a second their fingers stayed laced together.

"Coming?"

"Yeah."

They walked back toward the group, and the conversation folded around them. Laughter and stories and the easy banter of people who'd known each other for years.

By the time the fire started dying down and people began drifting away, she'd lost track of time. One by one, the blankets emptied. The cooler got packed up. Someone doused what was left of the flames with seawater.

"I'll walk you back," Ryan said.

They left the beach together, their footprints disappearing into the dark sand behind them. The jetty was a shadow at their backs now, and the town glowed ahead, distant and familiar.

They stopped where the beach met the street. The house was visible from here, lights on in the windows, the porch light left on for her.

"Thanks for walking me back," she said.

"Anytime." He paused. "You working the morning shift?"

"Unfortunately."

"I'll bring you a coffee. Black, right?"

She grinned. "You noticed."

"I notice things."

He took a step back. It looked like he might say something, or step closer, but he just smiled, lifted a hand, and turned back toward wherever he was going.

Brittany watched him until he disappeared into the dark, then walked home with sand in her shoes and woodsmoke in her hair.

* * *

The reading series at The Salty Grape wasn't the reason Lori had driven half an hour inland that evening. It was *a* reason. The history of barrier islands, the event John at Tidewater Books had mentioned when she'd browsed a few days ago, those were reasons too. But John himself, his voice when he'd said, "I hope you'll stop by." That was the reason she hadn't admitted to herself yet.

The Salty Grape looked nothing like the shore. A crushed-shell drive gave way to a converted stone barn with wide wooden doors propped open, string lights glowing against the fading sky. Beyond the main building, grapevines climbed neat trellises in rows that caught the last of the golden hour light. Someone had set up folding chairs on the flagstone patio out back, and maybe thirty people had already gathered, wine glasses in hand, the murmur of conversation mixing with the buzz of cicadas.

Lori got a glass of white at the bar and found a seat toward the middle. Not too close to the front, not hiding in the back. Casual.

John was near a small podium that had been set up by the stone wall, speaking with a man who must have been the evening's speaker. Sixties, white-bearded, wearing a faded polo shirt and khakis worn soft from fieldwork. John gestured toward the vineyard rows, said something that made the man laugh, then glanced out at the gathering crowd.

He caught her eye, or she thought he did. Lori raised her hand in an awkward half-wave before realizing he was looking past her. A woman brushed by from behind, making for the podium, and John greeted her with a hug.

Lori took a long sip of wine and studied the program.

The chairs filled in slowly. A couple sat down next to her, already mid-conversation about someone's daughter's wedding. An older woman claimed the seat on her other side and immediately began fanning herself with the program.

A gray hound mix with a grizzled muzzle wandered

between the rows, accepting pats from anyone who offered. It paused at Lori's chair, sniffed her ankle thoroughly, then sat down directly on her feet.

"Oh," Lori said. "Hello."

It looked up at her as if it had chosen her specifically and would not be moved.

She tried to shift her feet. The dog leaned harder against her shins.

The woman beside her glanced over. "Looks like you made a friend."

"Lucky me," Lori said, though the dog's weight was oddly comforting. Like a heavy, slightly smelly weighted blanket.

At seven on the dot, John stepped to the podium.

"Thank you all for coming," he said, and the patio quieted. "For those who don't know me, I'm John. I own Tidewater Books in Sea Isle, and a few years ago I started this series to bring together the people who understand this place best, not just writers, but historians, naturalists, anyone with something worth sharing." He looked out at the crowd. "Tonight, we're continuing with one of the best."

He introduced the speaker without notes. Dr. Scott Shiles, retired professor from Stockton, thirty years studying the ecology and history of New Jersey's barrier islands. Author of two books Lori had never heard of and now wanted to read.

"Scott knows more about this stretch of coastline than anyone I've ever met," John said. "And he tells it better than most novelists. So without further ado."

Scott took his place at the podium. He was smaller than he'd looked from a distance, but his voice carried easily across the patio, steady and warm and practiced.

He didn't start with facts. He started with a story.

September 1944. A hurricane that the locals still called the Great Atlantic Hurricane, though most history books had forgotten it. How the storm had reshaped the coastline, washing away what people thought was permanent. Boardwalks, piers, whole stretches of dune. How the beaches that everyone took for granted had been rebuilt by hand in the years after, crews of men with shovels planting beach grass one clump at a time. How the islands themselves were moving, always moving, sand shifting with every storm, the whole coastline slowly reshaping itself.

Lori forgot about her wine. Forgot about the uncomfortable folding chair, the heat that still hung in the evening air, even the dog on her feet.

She'd walked this beach a hundred times. She'd never thought of it as something that moved.

"Seventy-five miles," Scott said at one point, gesturing east. "That's how far out the coastline was during the last ice age. Past the continental shelf. When the glaciers melted, the sea rose nearly four hundred feet. Swallowed everything in its path. The barrier islands we see now? They're just the latest version. The ocean's been remaking this coast for ten thousand years."

He talked about the inlets that had opened and closed over centuries. Places where the ocean had simply punched through, rearranging the map until someone filled it back in. The forests that had once stood where the bay now sat, drowned when the sea level rose. The shipwrecks still buried in the sand offshore, and the hotels that had washed away in storms nobody remembered, and the way the coastline in old photographs bore no resemblance to what stood today.

"The shore isn't permanent," he said, near the end. "That's the thing people don't understand. We build on it like it's solid ground, but it's not. It's a negotiation. Between the land and the water, between what we want and what the ocean allows. And the ocean always wins eventually."

When he finished, the applause was warm and genuine, the sound of people who hadn't expected to learn something and had. One attendee asked about climate change and what it meant for the islands. Another asked about the best places to see the old foundations, whatever remained of them.

A man in the front row raised his hand. "Dr. Shiles, I have a question about the 1944 hurricane."

"Of course," Scott said.

"Do you think the government covered up the actual damage because of the war effort? Because I've been researching this, and the official reports seem inconsistent with eyewitness accounts I've found in my aunt's attic."

Scott blinked. "I... haven't encountered evidence of a cover-up, no. Though wartime reporting was certainly limited—"

"Because my aunt's neighbor's cousin was there, and she said the waves were sixty feet high. Sixty feet. That's not in any official record."

"Wave heights can be difficult to estimate in the moment—"

"I'm just saying. Something doesn't add up."

Scott nodded slowly, with the weary patience of a man who had fielded stranger questions in his career. "I'd be happy to look at any documents you've found. Primary sources are always valuable."

The dog, still planted on Lori's feet, chose this moment to let out a long, groaning sigh that expressed what everyone was thinking.

John moderated from the side, steering the questions back on track, stepping in when the conversation flagged. He caught Lori's eye once, briefly, and almost smiled.

She looked away first. Took a sip of the wine she'd forgotten she was holding.

After the Q&A, the formal part dissolved into mingling. People clustered around Scott, asking follow-up questions, mentioning properties they owned and whether they should be worried. Others made their way to the bar for refills. The sun had finally dropped below the tree line, and the string lights along the patio fence glowed brighter now against the darker sky.

She reached down and gave the dog a scratch behind the ears before getting to her feet. He gave her a reproachful look anyway, then wandered toward the refreshment table. She drifted to the far end of the patio, looking out at the vineyard rows. The vines were thick with new growth, small clusters of flowers just giving way to the hard green pinpricks of forming grapes.

"What did you think?"

John was beside her. He'd rolled up his sleeves against the heat, and she noticed for the first time a tattoo on his forearm, a compass rose, faded with age.

The dog had roused itself from under the refreshment table and was making its way toward them with determination. It sat down on Lori's feet again, reclaiming its territory.

John looked down at the dog then back at Lori. "That's Gus. He doesn't usually take to people this quickly."

"We bonded during the sixty-foot wave theory."

John grinned. "Ah. That was Maurice."

"The conspiracy guy?"

"Maurice Englebert. He comes to every event. Always has a theory." John rolled his eyes, but fondly. "He once asked a memoirist if she thought her childhood memories had been implanted by the CIA. She handled it beautifully."

Lori laughed, surprising herself.

"I think I need to buy his books," she said, nodding toward where Scott was still chatting with attendees.

"High praise."

"I had no idea. About any of it. The storm, the inlets—" She shook her head. "I've been coming to Sea Isle since I was a kid, and I never knew the island was actually moving."

"Most people don't. They see the beach and the houses and they think it's always been this way." He poured himself a glass from the bottle on the nearby table. "That's why I wanted to do this. Not just book readings, those are fine, but everyone does those. I wanted talks that made them see the place differently."

"Is that what the bookstore is for too?"

He smiled at that. "I opened the bookstore because I burned out on corporate life and needed work that mattered. But somewhere along the way it grew into more than a shop. It became about building a place where people could stumble onto things they didn't know they needed."

She turned her wine glass in her hands.

"What about you?" John asked. "What brings you to Sea Isle for the summer?"

"Friends. A group of us rented a house. Our kids are all around the same age, so it seemed like a good idea." A beat. "My son is seventeen. I'm not sure he'd use those words for it."

"Seventeen is a hard age."

"You have kids?"

"Two. Both grown now, living their own lives in cities I need a GPS to navigate." He lifted his glass. "They turned out fine despite everything. That's the only parenting metric I'm confident about."

That got a real smile out of her.

The crowd had thinned. Scott was packing up his notes, shaking hands with the last few people who'd lingered. Gus was sprawled under the refreshment table, twitching through some dream.

"I should let you close things out," Lori said.

"I should." But he lingered. "I'm glad you came. It means something, when new people find their way here."

"I'm glad I came too."

He turned to go then looked back. "We do these weekly. I've got a fisherman lined up in a few days—wrote a memoir about fifty years on these waters. Different topic, same idea." His eyes held hers. "If you're still around."

"I'll be here all summer."

"Then I hope to see you."

He returned to the podium, and Lori watched him go. The air had softened with dusk, carrying the green scent of the vineyard and something faintly sweet from the last of the day's heat. The knot in her shoulders had loosened without her noticing.

She was reaching for her bag when her phone buzzed.

Kevin, the screen said. Her ex-husband.

For a moment she considered not answering. Letting it ring through to voicemail, dealing with whatever it was later, when she wasn't standing in a vineyard feeling lighter than she had in months, something bright and unfamiliar just starting to take shape.

But Kevin never called without a reason.

She stepped away from the remaining guests and answered.

"Lori." Kevin's voice was clipped. "We need to talk about Ethan."

"What about him?"

"He still hasn't responded about the wedding. I need to finalize the groomsmen list by the end of the week, and he's the only one who hasn't given me an answer."

Lori pressed her free hand to her forehead. The air that had felt so pleasant a moment ago now hung heavy. "Have you tried calling him directly?"

"He doesn't answer my calls. You know that."

"Then maybe that's your answer."

Silence. When Kevin spoke again, his tone had hardened. "This is what I'm talking about."

"What's that supposed to mean?"

"You're poisoning him against me. You have been since the divorce. Every time I try to have a relationship with my son, you're there in the background, whispering in his ear—"

Poisoning. The accusation landed like a slap. She knew he used it on Ethan too—she'd heard it secondhand, filtered through a son who'd stopped talking.

"I haven't whispered anything." Lori kept her voice low, conscious of the people still mingling on the patio. "Ethan's not a child. He's capable of forming his own opinions. Maybe if you talked to him instead of at him—"

"I've tried talking to him. He shuts down. He walks away. He acts like I'm the enemy."

"And you think that's my fault?"

"I think you could help if you wanted to. You could tell him that being in my wedding isn't a betrayal. That supporting his father doesn't mean taking sides."

Lori's jaw ached. She'd been clenching it. "Kevin, I can't make him feel something he doesn't feel."

"You could try."

"He's dealing with a lot right now. The divorce, the engagement—"

"The engagement happened six months ago. He's had time."

"Time doesn't work like that."

"Meaning what, exactly?"

"It means you can't put a deadline on grief."

Kevin exhaled sharply. "This isn't grief, Lori. This is stubbornness. This is a seventeen-year-old being difficult because he knows he can get away with it. And if you won't help me reach him, then I'll have to do it myself."

"What does that mean?"

"I'm coming down there. This weekend. I'll talk to him face-to-face, and we'll settle this once and for all."

The air went out of her. "You're not—Kevin, you can't just show up."

"He's my son."

"And I'm his mother. And we're on vacation. This isn't the time."

"The wedding is coming up fast. When exactly would be the time?"

She didn't have an answer for that.

"I'll text you when I'm on my way," Kevin said. "Make sure he's there."

He hung up before she could respond.

Lori stood among the vines, phone still pressed to her ear, listening to nothing. Around her, the evening continued. Guests drifting to their cars, laughter floating from the patio, the soft crunch of shells underfoot. The string lights swayed slightly in the breeze, and somewhere in the fields a bird called out and went quiet.

Back on the patio, John was stacking chairs. Scott was loading a box of books into his car. The night had felt so full of possibility. Now it was just a night.

She thought about going back. Thanking John for the event. Lingering a little longer in that other version of the night, the one where Kevin hadn't called, where she was just a woman at a vineyard, learning about barrier islands.

But the call had happened. Kevin was coming. And she'd have to go to the house and figure out how to tell Ethan.

She walked to her car with her hands in her pockets, the evening's warmth already fading.

CHAPTER EIGHT

Carrie had claimed the beach chair closest to the dunes, laptop balanced on her knees, the glow of the screen washed out by the sun overhead.

She had three tabs open: her email, waiting for Gayle's name to appear with news about the motion to delay; LinkedIn, where she'd finally added the freelance bookkeeping clients she'd picked up over the years; and a job listing for a full-time accounting position at a property management company back home. The posting had been up for six days. She'd written and rewritten her cover letter twice already, trying to make fifteen years of part-time gigs and volunteer treasurer roles sound like a coherent career instead of what they were, the scraps Richard had left her when he decided there was "no room" for her at the company she'd helped build. She deleted the line about her business background and tried again.

Beside her, Jen had her laptop out, fingers moving in quick bursts. She'd broken through on the Clementine Fields draft two days ago and hadn't stopped since. Pages coming faster than they had in months, the ending finally taking shape after all those stalled weeks. She'd mentioned it to the group over tacos on the deck, downplaying it the way she always did, but Meredith had seen the relief underneath. Almost done.

Olivia came out of the water, dripping, goggles pushed up onto her forehead. She'd been doing laps along the shoreline for the better part of an hour, far enough out that the waves barely broke. She grabbed her towel and dropped onto the sheet beside Lori, who was pretending to read the book John had recommended while actually watching Ethan.

He was down the beach with Max, the two of them tossing a football in lazy arcs. Not talking, just throwing and catching. Ethan had been quite a bit less withdrawn since he'd started at The Crabby Catch. Not transformed, but present.

"He looks better," Meredith said, settling into her chair with her iced coffee.

"He's getting there," Lori said. "This place is good for him. I think."

Sophie and Brittany had set up closer to the water. Sophie was texting Trevor again. She'd been on her phone constantly since they arrived. Brittany lay on her stomach, scrolling through something that looked like homework. Ava was farther down the beach with her camera, photographing the lifeguard stand or the waves or whatever had caught her eye.

"Paddle ball?" Max jogged over from where he'd been with Ethan, holding two wooden paddles and a ball. "Anyone? Come on, it's the beach. Someone has to play paddle ball."

"Not me," Lily said, eyes still on her book.

"You never do anything."

"I do plenty of things. They just don't involve paddles."

"Sophie?" Max turned his attention to the other towel setup. "Brittany? Come on, one of you."

Sophie glanced at her phone then set it down. "Fine. But I'm rusty."

"Nobody's rusty at paddle ball. It's paddle ball."

They headed for the firmer sand near the water, and soon

the steady thwack of the ball joined the soundtrack of the morning.

The hours slid by. Reading, napping, the occasional trip to the water, someone making a Wawa run for drinks and coming back with three times what anyone had asked for. By late afternoon, the crowd had thinned and the lifeguards were pulling in the flags, and everyone was ready for showers and the promise of evening.

They packed up slowly. Sophie and Brittany headed back first, claiming showers before the rush. Ethan was the last to leave, taking his time folding his towel, lingering.

Lori waited until he was out of earshot. "Kevin's coming this weekend. To talk to Ethan about the wedding."

Olivia looked up. "He told you that?"

"Told. Announced. Demanded I make sure Ethan was available." She shouldered her beach bag. "I haven't figured out how to tell him yet."

"Tell Ethan, or tell Kevin no?" Meredith asked.

"Either. Both." She started toward the dunes.

* * *

Tom had volunteered to stay with the teens. Burgers on the grill, a movie in the living room, the promise that he wouldn't try too hard to be cool. By nine o'clock, Ocean Drive was already packed.

The OD was everything a shore bar should be. Dark, loud, and a little sticky. The dance floor filled the center of the main room, three bars surrounding it, bodies already pressing in even though the cover band hadn't started yet. The ceiling hung low, old wood paneling that had seen decades of hands slapping against it in time with the music. The whole place smelled like spilled beer and sunscreen and something vaguely fried from the kitchen. A guy near the door was checking IDs and collecting the cover, a tip jar already stuffed with ones.

The five of them pushed through to the back bar. They were easily the oldest people in the room by twenty years, and nobody cared, least of all them.

"Two pitchers of whatever's on draft," Meredith said to the bartender, a guy in his twenties with a backwards Phillies cap and a patient expression. "And five glasses."

"Cash only," he said.

Meredith pulled a twenty from her pocket. "I remember."

"Also some waters," Olivia added. "For later. Hydration is important."

"You sound like my doctor," Lori said.

"Your doctor is correct."

They found a spot along the wall where they could actually hear each other.

"Man, this place hasn't changed," Carrie said, looking around. She'd changed three times before leaving the house, settling at last on a sundress she hadn't worn since before the divorce. "It's exactly the same."

"That's the point," Jen said. "That's why people keep coming back."

The band started their first set with a nineties cover that made Jen laugh out loud. "Oh, come on. We danced to this at Rowan."

"We danced to everything at Rowan," Olivia said. "We had no standards."

"We had excellent standards," Jen shot back. "We just also had no inhibitions."

The music was good, if predictable. Classic rock, some newer stuff, a crowd-pleasing setlist designed to keep people ordering drinks and staying late. By the second song, half the crowd was on their feet, and by the third, Lori had dragged Carrie onto the dance floor despite her protests.

Meredith stayed at the table, holding her beer without drinking, watching her friends move. It had been years since they'd done this, really done it, not just dinner and conversation but actually going out, being loud, dancing like they were twenty-two again. They'd all gotten so careful. So measured. So focused on managing everything that they'd forgotten how to just be.

Olivia leaned in beside her. "You're thinking too hard."

"I'm not thinking at all."

"You have your organizing face on. The one that means you're cataloging everyone's energy levels and calculating when we should leave."

Meredith laughed. "Maybe a little."

"Stop. For once, just stop." Olivia reached for her glass. "We have tonight. Tom's handling the teens. Nobody needs us to be anywhere or do anything. When was the last time that happened?"

Meredith considered. "I don't remember."

"Exactly."

Nearby, Jen had joined Carrie and Lori on the dance floor. The band launched into a faster track, and someone near the stage let out a whoop that sent ripples of laughter through the crowd.

"Fine," Meredith said. "But if I pull something, you're explaining it to Tom."

"Deal."

They joined the others, five women in their mid-forties who had stopped caring what anyone thought of them. The songs blurred together, one into the next, familiar and unfamiliar, music that didn't ask anything of you. Around them, younger people were reaching up to slap the low ceiling in time with the beat, an OD tradition that never seemed to die. At some point, the lead singer made a joke about the crowd's energy, and Lori yelled something back that made him laugh into the microphone.

A younger woman near them, maybe twenty-five with blond highlights and a complicated-looking cocktail, leaned over to Carrie. "You guys are goals. Seriously."

Carrie blinked. "We are?"

"My mom's book club never goes out like this. They just drink wine and complain about their husbands."

"Honey," Jen called over, "we do both. We're multitaskers."

The woman laughed and raised her glass in their direction before being pulled away by her friends. Carrie watched her go.

"What?" Meredith asked.

"Nothing. Just—" She shook her head. "Nothing. I'm going to get more water."

She headed for the bar, but Meredith noticed she was smiling.

Between sets, they grabbed water and more beer. Carrie's cheeks were flushed, her hair escaping from its clip in ways she would have fixed an hour ago. Jen was grinning like she used to when every weekend felt like an adventure. Even Olivia seemed lighter, the tension in her shoulders gone for once.

"Remember junior year?" Lori said, wiping her forehead with a bar napkin. "That bar near campus, the one with the terrible wings and the DJ who only played house music?"

"Main St.," Jen supplied. "We practically lived there."

"We definitely shouldn't have," Lori said.

"The wings gave me food poisoning twice," Olivia said. "And I kept going back."

"Because the bouncer never checked IDs," Carrie said.

"Because we were young and stupid," Meredith corrected. "We didn't need better reasons."

The conversation wound back through shared history. The time Lori accidentally set off the fire alarm in the dorm, the road trip to the Shore that ended with Jen's car on the side of the Parkway, the night before graduation when they'd promised to stay friends and then actually done it.

"Twenty-seven years," Carrie said. "That's a long time."

"Longer than most marriages," Lori said.

"I forgot this," Carrie said, pressing a cold glass to her forehead. "I forgot we could do this."

"You didn't forget," Lori said. "You just stopped."

They drifted out to the Sandbar, hoping for air, but it was just as packed. People crowded around the outdoor bar, sand underfoot.

They'd barely found a spot when Lori grabbed Meredith's arm and ducked behind her.

"What are you doing?" Meredith asked.

"Don't turn around. Whatever you do, don't—"

Naturally, everyone turned around.

John had just stepped out onto the Sandbar, scanning the crowd. He wore a chambray button-down untucked over jeans, his ponytail loose against his collar. A woman Meredith didn't recognize was beside him. Fifties, silver earrings, put together in a way that looked effortless.

"Oh wow, is that him?" Jen craned her neck. "The bookstore guy?"

"Stop looking!" Lori was trying to make herself smaller, which wasn't easy when you were five-eight. "Why is he here? He doesn't seem like the OD type."

"Maybe he contains multitudes," Olivia said. "Who's the woman?"

Lori peered around Meredith's shoulder. John and his companion had found a spot near the bar, their heads bent together in conversation. "I don't know. She looks like she has her life figured out."

"So do you," Carrie said.

"I'm sweaty and my hair is doing something tragic and I have beer on my shirt." Lori looked down. "When did I get beer on my shirt?"

"You look great," Meredith said. "Like you've been having fun. That's allowed."

"I didn't want him to see me like this. I wanted—" She

stopped, shook her head. "I don't know what I wanted. I hadn't gotten that far."

"You like him," Jen said.

"I barely know him. I've talked to him twice. Three times if you count buying a book."

"And yet here you are, hiding behind Meredith," Jen said.

Lori straightened up, attempting dignity. "I'm not hiding. I'm just... not making myself obvious."

"Honey, you're the opposite of obvious right now," Jen said. "You're acting like a teenager."

"I'm aware." She risked another look toward the bar. John was laughing at something the woman had said, his whole face animated. "She's probably his girlfriend. Or his wife. Someone like him doesn't stay single."

"You don't know that," Carrie said.

"I don't know anything. That's the problem."

Inside, the band started their second set, the music drifting out through the open doors. Lori was still watching John, trying to look like she wasn't watching John, when he glanced up and caught her eye.

For a moment, neither of them moved. Then he smiled—a real smile, warm and surprised—and raised his glass in her direction before turning back to his companion.

Lori whipped around to face the group, her cheeks flushed. "Did that just happen?"

"That happened," Olivia confirmed.

"What do I do?"

"Wave back? Go say hi? Act like a normal human being?" Olivia suggested.

"I can't go over there. She's right there." Lori pressed her hands to her face. "I need a minute. I'm going to the bathroom."

She was gone before anyone could respond, weaving through the crowd toward the back of the bar.

Jen watched her go. "Should someone...?"

"Give her a minute," Meredith said. "She'll be fine."

But after a few minutes, Jen went anyway. Meredith and Olivia and Carrie stood in the warm night air, the bass from inside thrumming through the sand beneath their feet.

"She really likes him," Carrie said.

Meredith nodded. "I know."

Carrie shook her head. "I haven't seen her like this since... I don't even know. Before Kevin, maybe. Before everything went sideways."

"She's scared," Meredith said. "You can't blame her."

"I don't blame her," Carrie said. "I just hope she doesn't talk herself out of it before she even gives it a chance."

Jen came back with Lori a few minutes later. Lori had splashed water on her face and fixed her hair, and she seemed calmer, more like herself.

"I'm fine," she said before anyone could ask. "I was being ridiculous. He's allowed to have drinks with whoever he wants. I barely know him."

"You could go say hello," Carrie offered.

"I could. But I'm not going to walk up to a man I find attractive and make small talk while his date watches. I have some pride left."

"We don't know she's his date," Meredith said.

"We don't know she's not."

The band finished their song, and the lead singer announced a fifteen-minute break. The music cut out, and suddenly they could hear themselves think again. Lori glanced toward where John had been standing.

He was walking toward them.

Lori saw it the same moment everyone else did. She went still.

"Ladies," John said, stopping in front of them. "I thought I recognized you." He was looking at Lori. "I didn't expect to see you here."

"Likewise." Lori's voice was steadier than she felt. "We were just—celebrating. Old times. College nostalgia."

"The band's good for that." He glanced back toward where his companion was waiting, checking her phone. "That's my sister. She's visiting from Portland for the week. I promised her a night out that didn't involve me talking about books."

"Your sister," Lori repeated.

"Jill. She's a pediatric surgeon. Considerably more impressive than I am at dinner parties." He smiled. "I should get back. But I'm glad I ran into you. The fisherman talk is in a few days, if you're still interested."

"I am. I'll be there."

"Good." He nodded to the rest of the group and headed back to his sister.

Nobody said anything.

"His sister," Carrie said.

Lori laughed. "His sister."

"You're an idiot," Jen said affectionately.

"Shut up."

But she was smiling now, really smiling, and when the band came back for their final set, she was the first one on the dance floor.

* * *

They closed out the bar.

The walk back was long and loud, all of them taking up the entire sidewalk, singing fragments of songs they'd been dancing to, stopping every few blocks to catch their breath or point out something in a shop window. The night had cooled just enough to feel comfortable, and Sea Isle had gone quiet the way beach towns do when the families go to bed and only the stragglers remain.

By the time they reached 59th Street, Meredith's feet ached and her voice was hoarse and she didn't care about either.

"That was fun," she said, as the house came into view. "That was really fun."

"We should do it again," Carrie said. "Before the summer ends. Make it a thing."

"Make it a thing," Olivia echoed. "I like that."

The house was still when they came through the door. Tom was asleep on the couch with the TV still on, the teens presumably in their rooms, the only sound the distant crash of waves through the open windows. They separated with whispered goodnights, Lori and Carrie heading upstairs, Jen into the kitchen for water, Meredith gently waking Tom to guide him up to bed.

Olivia stood in the hallway, keys still in her hand, not quite ready to go upstairs.

The night had been good. Better than good. For three hours she hadn't thought about Dan, hadn't checked her phone, hadn't wondered what Michael was doing or whether she should call him back. She'd just been herself. She'd forgotten that was allowed.

She wanted to hold onto that feeling. Wanted to carry it upstairs and fall asleep before it faded.

But as she turned toward the stairs, she noticed the light.

Lily's door, cracked open, the soft glow of a reading lamp visible through the gap.

It was nearly one in the morning. Lily was a night owl, but this was late even for her.

Olivia hesitated. The beer was still in her system, making everything feel removed and dreamlike. She pushed the door open instead of walking past.

Lily was sitting up in bed, book open in her lap, but she wasn't reading. She was staring at the wall, her dark hair loose around her shoulders, her expression distant. In the soft lamplight, she looked younger than fifteen, the way she was worrying the corner of a page, her knees pulled up to her chest.

"Hey," Olivia said. "You're up late."

Lily looked up, eyes startled. "Couldn't sleep."

"Want to talk about it?"

A pause. Then: "Not really."

Olivia should have left it there. Should have said goodnight and gone to her own room and dealt with whatever this was in the morning, when she was sober and clearheaded and better equipped for difficult conversations.

But Lily was just sitting there. Waiting.

Olivia crossed to the bed and sat on the edge, leaving space between them. "What's going on?"

Lily didn't answer. Her eyes stayed on the wall.

"I thought maybe it was just being fifteen. Or being away from home." Olivia kept her voice even. "But it's more than that. Isn't it."

Silence.

"What is it?"

"You're going to be upset."

"Maybe. But I'd rather know than wonder."

More silence. Somewhere outside, a car door closed. Footsteps on a neighboring porch, then quiet again.

"It was in January," Lily said at last. "Before you and Dad started acting weird. Before you stopped talking to each other at dinner."

January. A month before Olivia had found the texts.

"I couldn't sleep," Lily continued. "I kept having these dreams about—it doesn't matter. Anyway, I went downstairs to get water, and I heard a car pull up outside."

Olivia's heart had started to beat in a strange, arrhythmic way.

"It was late. Like, two in the morning. I looked out the window because I thought maybe someone was picking something up, or there was an Uber, or—I don't know what I thought."

She stopped. Olivia waited.

"Dad was outside." The words came out flat now, rehearsed, like she'd been waiting to say them. "He walked out to the car. A woman got out. They kissed. For a long time. Like, really kissed. And then they talked for a while, and she got back in her car, and Dad came back inside."

Olivia could feel the beer souring in her stomach.

"I went back to bed," Lily said. "I convinced myself I'd imagined it. Or that it was someone else. Or that I'd been sleepwalking and dreaming the whole thing." She finally looked at Olivia, and her eyes were wet. "But I know what I saw. I've known for months."

"Why didn't you tell me?"

"Because I was scared." Her voice broke. "I was scared that if I said something, you'd get divorced. That everything would fall apart. And I kept thinking maybe I was wrong, maybe I didn't see what I thought I saw, maybe Dad just—"

"Just what?"

"I don't know." Lily wiped her eyes with the back of her hand. "I kept hoping it would go away. That things would get better. That I wouldn't have to say anything."

Olivia didn't move. Everything she'd told herself since February—that Dan had made a mistake, that they could fix it, that she could forgive—was falling apart.

Dan had kissed Rachel.

Physically. Actually. In the middle of the night, in front of their house, while their daughter watched from a window.

He'd looked her in the eye and sworn it was only emotional. Only texts. Nothing physical.

And she'd believed him. She'd wanted to believe him.

"Mom?" Lily looked up at her. "Are you okay?"

Olivia reached for her daughter's hand and held it. Her own hands weren't shaking, which surprised her.

"I'm glad you told me," she said. "I know that was hard."

"Are you going to leave him?"

"I need to think," Olivia said. "I need—"

She didn't finish the sentence. Didn't know how to finish it.

Lily was crying now, and Olivia pulled her close the way she used to when Lily was small and scared of the dark. Held her until she was still.

"You should sleep," Olivia said eventually. "We'll talk more tomorrow."

"What are you going to do?"

She kissed the top of Lily's head. "Whatever happens, it's not your fault. None of this is your fault. Do you understand?"

"But if I hadn't said anything——"

"Lily. Look at me." Olivia waited until her daughter's eyes met hers. "I already knew something was wrong. I found some texts back in February. Dad and I have been... working through things. So this isn't you telling me something I didn't know. It's you telling me something I needed to hear. Okay?"

Lily stared at her. "You already knew?"

"Not what you saw. But I knew there was a problem." She squeezed Lily's hand. "You didn't break anything. I promise."

Lily nodded, though she still seemed shaky.

Olivia stood. Walked to the door.

"Mom?"

She turned.

"I'm sorry I didn't tell you sooner."

"I'm sorry you had to carry it at all," Olivia said.

She closed the door behind her and stood in the hallway, listening to the sounds of the sleeping house. Somewhere down the hall, someone's phone buzzed against a nightstand. The refrigerator hummed in the kitchen. Outside, the waves kept coming.

Dan had lied. He'd looked at her across a marriage counselor's office and sworn that nothing physical had happened. And the whole time, he'd been lying.

She walked to her own room and sat on the bed without turning on the light.

Her phone was on the nightstand. Three texts from Dan, sent hours ago, still unanswered.

Miss you. Hope you had fun tonight.

The house feels empty without you.

Call me when you can. Just want to hear your voice.

She stared at the words until they blurred. Then she turned the phone over and lay back.

She thought about Michael. How he looked at her. How he listened. How she'd felt on that trail at Cape May, guilty but also alive.

She'd been torturing herself over a few hikes and some texts that never crossed any lines. Meanwhile, Dan had been crossing every line there was and making her feel like the one with something to apologize for.

Then the anger hit.

She welcomed it. She'd spent so long trying to understand, to forgive, to be the bigger person. And for what?

For a man who couldn't even give her the truth.

She picked up her phone again. Not Dan's texts this time. Michael's. She typed *Hey*, then deleted it. Set the phone down. Closed her eyes.

CHAPTER NINE

Carrie arrived at Excursion Park while the vendors were still setting up. Trucks backed up to tent spaces along the path, crates coming off tailgates, the morning light warm and soft. A coffee cart had claimed a spot near the entrance, and a couple walked past with beach chairs under their arms, already staking their claim on the day.

Marge was at the Saltmeadow tent, unloading crates from Frank's truck. "You're early," she said. "Good."

They set up together—strawberries first, then sugar snap peas, zucchini, fresh herbs bundled with twine. Marge showed her where everything went, which bins to keep full, how to arrange the display so customers could see the best produce first.

"I'm going to check on the honey guy," Marge said once the display was set. "You good here?"

Carrie hesitated then nodded.

By eight, the market opened and customers started trickling in. Carrie answered questions, made change, chatted about the weather.

Around nine, Mrs. Dougherty arrived for her strawberries.

She came every week, seventy-something and sharp-eyed, with opinions about everything and a voice that carried.

"These look good," she said, examining a quart of berries with the focus of a jeweler. "Better than the last batch."

"We got lucky this week," Carrie said, straightening the display.

"You're new." Mrs. Dougherty selected two quarts and set them on the counter. "You weren't here last summer."

"First time. I'm staying in Sea Isle for a few months."

"Lucky you." The older woman pulled a twenty from her purse. "A whole summer at the shore. That's something."

"It is," Carrie said. She believed that now.

After Mrs. Dougherty left, the morning continued. Customers came and went, questions she was learning to answer. By midmorning, the rush had tapered off.

She was restocking the strawberry display when her phone buzzed in her back pocket.

She almost ignored it. The morning was too good to interrupt with whatever fresh anxiety was waiting in her inbox. But habit won out. She set the crate on the counter and pulled out her phone.

Gayle Brown. Her divorce attorney.

Business valuation came back. Your contributions were significantly higher than Richard claimed. This changes everything. Call me when you can.

Carrie stared at the words. Read them again.

She didn't cry. She'd thought she might, if this moment ever came.

A voice nearby was asking about tomatoes.

"Excuse me? The tomatoes?"

She blinked. Turned. A man in a fishing hat was pointing at the nearly empty tomato section.

"Not yet," she managed. "Another few weeks."

He nodded and moved on.

She put the phone back in her pocket and finished with the strawberries.

When Marge stopped back by, she stood watching for a moment.

"You look different," she said.

Carrie smiled. "Good different?"

"You tell me."

"Good different," Carrie said. "Definitely good different."

* * *

Carrie sat in her car after the market ended, parked in the shade on a side street, and called Gayle. For twenty minutes she'd listened to numbers that rewrote the story of her marriage. Not dramatically. Just enough. Enough to matter.

By the time she pulled into the driveway, the conversation was still replaying in her head.

The front door was unlocked. She stepped into the entryway and heard voices from the living room, but not the usual sounds.

These voices were tense.

Carrie stopped in the hallway, keys still in her hand.

"I don't understand why this has to be so difficult." A man's voice, smooth and practiced, already impatient. "All I'm asking for is a conversation."

"We had a conversation." That was Ethan. Lower, harder, the anger barely contained. "I said I'd think about it."

"That was two months ago."

Carrie moved toward the living room, her footsteps soft on the hardwood.

The scene arranged itself as she reached the doorway. Kevin stood near the windows, dressed in expensive casual clothes. She hadn't seen him since Lori's divorce, but he looked the same—polished, confident, filling the room with his presence whether anyone wanted him to or not.

Tom was on the couch, playing the host while watching everything. Ethan stood near the kitchen doorway, jaw tight, arms rigid, looking like he wanted to be anywhere else.

"Carrie." Tom's voice broke the tension, or at least redirected it. "Good timing. Can I get you something? Iced tea?"

"I'm fine." She stayed where she was. "What's going on?"

Kevin turned to her with a smile he probably practiced in mirrors. "Just a family discussion. Nothing to worry about."

"It's not a discussion," Ethan said. "You just showed up. Without telling anyone."

"I told your mother I was coming."

"You told her you might come this weekend. It's not the weekend."

"Plans changed." Kevin's composure was impressive, Carrie had to admit. Like a politician smiling through a scandal. "I had some free time, and I thought, why wait? Why not drive down and see my son?"

"You thought wrong." Ethan didn't blink.

The room went quiet. Carrie could hear the ocean through the open windows, the distant sound of kids on the beach, the everyday summer sounds that suddenly felt very far away.

Tom stood slowly. "Maybe we should—"

"Stay out of this." Kevin's voice hardened. "This is between me and my son."

"I'm only your son when it's convenient." Ethan's hands curled into fists. "You can't just appear and expect everything to be fine."

"I'm not asking for that. I'm asking you to be in my wedding."

"Same thing." Ethan didn't look away.

Kevin took a breath. "Ethan. I'm still your father. When I get married, I want my son standing next to me."

"You mean Tessa wants everyone smiling for the cameras like we're one big happy family."

Kevin's face flickered. "That's not—"

"I heard you on the phone with her. 'It'll look better if he's there.' That's what you said." Ethan's voice cracked. "You don't actually care if I'm okay with it. You just need me to show up so everyone thinks we're fine."

"That's not fair."

"None of this is fair." His voice rose. "You think I wanted to spend every other weekend pretending I'm fine with your girl-friend making me smoothies? You think I didn't figure out the timeline? You introduced me to her three months after you left."

Kevin opened his mouth. "If your mother hadn't—"

"Don't." Ethan's voice went hard. "She didn't do anything. This is just how I feel. You moved on. I didn't. And you can't make me."

Silence.

Tom stepped between them. "Maybe this isn't the time. Everyone's emotions are running high. Give it a few days—"

"A few days?" Kevin turned to him, the smooth facade cracking. "So my son's mother has more time to work on him? So he can have more therapy sessions to convince him I'm the villain?"

"That's not what I said."

"You don't get to tell me how to handle my family." Kevin stepped toward Tom, close enough that Carrie's pulse spiked. "This is between me and my son."

Tom didn't move. "Ethan's a minor, and he's clearly upset. That concerns everyone in this house."

"He's my son." Kevin's voice dropped.

"And he's asking you to leave."

The standoff held. Then the front door opened, and Lori walked in with grocery bags in both hands.

She stopped just inside the door, taking in the scene. Carrie watched her shut down.

"Kevin." Her voice was flat. "I didn't realize you were coming today."

"I had an opening." He didn't take his eyes off Tom. "I came to talk to our son. Apparently that's not allowed anymore."

Lori set the grocery bags on the floor, moving slowly. "What happened?"

"Nothing happened." Kevin finally turned to face her. "I came to discuss the wedding, and I got a lecture from him"—he jerked his head toward Tom—"about how to parent my own child."

"I didn't lecture anyone," Tom said mildly. "I suggested we all take a breath."

"And I'm suggesting you stay out of it."

Lori looked at Ethan. He nodded slightly. Then she turned to Kevin.

"Ethan's allowed to have feelings, Kevin. That's not me. That's him."

"Right. Because nothing that comes out of his mouth has anything to do with what you've been telling him for three years."

"I haven't told him anything."

"You didn't have to. You made it clear with every silence, every sigh, every time you looked at me like I was something you scraped off your shoe." Kevin's voice had gone sharp, the polish falling away. "You think I don't know what you've been doing? Turning him against me piece by piece? Making sure he picks your side?"

Lori's voice stayed level. "There are no sides. There's just Ethan."

"There's always sides. And you made sure he picked yours."

Lori stood perfectly still, giving him nothing.

"If that were true," Lori said, "why would he be standing here listening to you instead of walking away?"

Kevin had no answer for that.

"Just go." Ethan's voice had steadied. "We can talk when you actually want to hear what I have to say."

"I came here to listen."

"No. You came to get what you want. Like always."

Kevin glanced around the room, at the faces watching him. For a moment he seemed almost human—hurt, confused, realizing he couldn't charm or argue his way to the outcome he wanted.

Then it was gone.

"Fine." He straightened his collar, a gesture so practiced it was probably unconscious. "We'll figure this out later. But this isn't over."

He walked to the door, pausing long enough to look at Lori one more time.

"This is what you wanted, isn't it? Him choosing you over me. Congratulations."

The door slammed behind him—harder than necessary, whether by accident or on purpose.

Nobody moved.

Ethan dropped onto the couch, pulling out his phone without looking at anyone. Carrie gathered the groceries and retreated to the kitchen; Tom waited, then settled on the opposite end of the couch, saying nothing.

After a minute, Ethan stood. "I'm going to the pool," he said to no one in particular.

Tom nodded. "Max is out there."

Ethan left through the side door. Tom caught Carrie's eye and tilted his head toward the deck. "I'll give you some space," he said, and stepped outside.

A moment later, Lori followed Carrie into the kitchen, moving on autopilot, her body going through motions while her mind caught up.

Carrie started putting groceries away.

At the counter, Lori leaned back and covered her face.

"I wasn't here," she said, muffled through her fingers. "I should have been here, and I wasn't."

"You couldn't have known." Carrie didn't stop moving, hands finding the right cabinets.

"I should have known. Kevin always does this. Shows up when he's not expected, makes himself the victim, walks away acting like everyone wronged him." She dropped her hands. She wasn't crying, but she was close. "I knew he'd pull something like this."

"He handled it," Carrie said.

"He shouldn't have to handle it. He's seventeen. This isn't his job."

Carrie didn't have a response for that, because Lori was right.

Carrie finished with the groceries and turned to face her friend. "He said it. The thing you've been holding back—about Kevin moving on while Ethan's still trying to figure out how to live with what happened." She leaned against the opposite counter. "You couldn't say it. He could."

Lori inhaled sharply. "Part of me is glad," she admitted, her voice small.

"That's not nothing."

"No. It's not."

They stood in silence. Carrie thought about her own morning, the text from Gayle, the validation she'd needed for longer than she wanted to admit.

"For what it's worth," Carrie said, "Tom was good with Kevin. Didn't escalate, didn't take sides. Just held the line."

"I noticed." Lori almost smiled. "Meredith picked a good one."

The deck door opened, and Meredith appeared. She'd missed the confrontation, but she'd heard enough.

"You okay?" Meredith asked.

Lori managed a small nod. "Getting there."

"The girls are coming back from the beach in about an hour. Do you want me to handle dinner?"

Lori shook her head. "You don't have to—"

"I know I don't have to. Do you want me to?"

Lori nodded, some of the tension going out of her.

Meredith headed upstairs, already pulling out her phone—ordering pizza, most likely.

* * *

Tom was on the deck when Lori finally went outside. The afternoon was fading, the light turning gold. He went back into the house, leaving her alone.

She'd checked the pool before coming out. Ethan was in the water with Max, not talking, just floating. She caught his eye; he looked away. Close enough.

She stayed there, looking out at the beach. The day crowd had thinned, replaced by the evening walkers and the die-hard sunbathers trying to squeeze the last light from the sky. A few surfers were out, catching small waves near the jetty. Down the beach, someone was flying a kite.

Meredith stepped out onto the deck and joined her at the railing without saying anything.

"You don't have to say anything," Lori said.

"I wasn't planning to."

They watched the water.

"When does it stop?" Lori asked. "The divorce was three years ago. And it's still not over. There's always something else."

"It ends when you stop giving Kevin so much power over you."

"One more year," Lori said. "Then Ethan's eighteen and Kevin can't use him as a pawn anymore."

"That's worth holding onto."

"It's everything."

They stayed there until the sun touched the horizon, until the sky started its slow fade from gold to rose to purple.

Ethan appeared at the deck stairs, towel over his shoulder.

He didn't say anything at first, just walked over and stood next to his mother.

Lori reached out and touched his arm. He let her.

The three of them watched the last light leave the sky. Ethan didn't apologize for the blowup. Lori didn't push him to talk.

After a while, Meredith went back inside, leaving them alone.

"I meant it," Ethan said quietly. "What I said to him."

"I know."

"He's not going to hear it."

"Maybe not." She looked at him. "But you said it anyway, and you meant it. That counts for something."

He nodded.

"I don't know if I can do the wedding," he said. "Stand up there and smile while he marries her."

"You don't have to decide yet." Lori kept her voice steady.

"He wants an answer."

"He can wait."

Ethan's shoulders loosened.

"Thanks for not being there," he said.

"What?"

"When he showed up. I'm glad you weren't there at first. I needed to say it without worrying about—" He stopped. "I don't know. You." He paused. "Tom helped. He didn't take over, but he was just... there. Like Kevin couldn't get past him."

Lori swallowed. "I'm sorry I wasn't there."

"Don't be. It worked out better this way."

She wanted to argue, but she stopped herself. He was telling her something important: he could handle more than she thought. He needed space to fight his own battles.

He might actually be okay.

* * *

Sophie didn't know anything was wrong until she got home.

At The Crabby Catch, it had been a normal shift. Busy enough to keep her moving, slow enough to catch her breath between rushes. Jake was working the patio again, and they'd started reading each other over the past week. He'd catch her eye when a difficult table finally left. She'd mouth good luck when a party of eight walked in without a reservation. Small things. Nothing that meant anything.

Except they did. She was starting to notice.

The trouble started at seven-thirty.

"We can't sit here." The woman gestured at the table Sophie had led them to. "It's right under the vent. I'll freeze."

Sophie smiled, apologized, found them another table.

"This one's too cramped. We'll be bumping elbows with the people next to us."

Another table. Another apology.

"This chair wobbles."

Sophie checked the floor. "I'm sorry, we're full right now, but I can grab a—"

"Forget it." The woman sat down hard. "Just get us some bread. We've been waiting."

They'd been seated for two minutes.

Sophie escaped back to the host stand, but she could feel the woman watching her.

When the entrées arrived and her salmon was "overcooked," the woman spotted Sophie across the restaurant.

"You." She pointed, voice rising. Now other customers turned to look. "You're the one who sat us at three different tables. Get me a manager." She was nearly shouting.

Jake got there first.

"I'm so sorry about your evening," he said, already picking up the plate. "Let me have the kitchen redo that salmon for you, on us. And I'll bring a round of drinks for the table while you wait."

The woman's husband finally looked up from his phone. "That works. Thank you."

Jake headed for the kitchen. Diane caught Sophie's eye and nodded toward the back. "Take five," Diane said. "Go get some air."

She went out the back door and stood in the alley, breathing in the smell of dumpsters and brine. Her hands were shaking.

It opened. Jake.

"You okay?"

"I don't know why I'm so shaken up."

"She was looking for a fight before she sat down. Nothing you could do was going to fix that." He leaned against the wall beside her. "Diane says you can head out early if you want."

"Yeah," Sophie said. "I should probably go."

They walked back inside together. Sophie grabbed her bag and said goodbye to Diane.

Jake was waiting by the back door. "I'm heading out too. I'll walk you."

They cut through the alley to the street. The evening had cooled, the promenade crowds thinning to couples and dog walkers.

"Thank you," she said. "For earlier. With Salmon Lady."

"Salmon Lady." He laughed. "That's what we're calling her?"

"In my head, forever."

He stopped beside a bike chained outside the surf shop. Old, a little rusty. "You want a ride? Handlebars. It's faster than walking."

She had a boyfriend. She should have said no.

Instead she said, "If I fall off, I'm blaming you."

She climbed on, gripping the metal bar on either side. Jake pushed off, wobbly at first, then steadier. The wind hit her face. She could feel him behind her, his arms on either side as he steered. It was ridiculous and probably unsafe, and she started laughing.

"Right here," she said.

"I know where you're staying."

Sophie raised an eyebrow. "That's creepy."

"You told me. First week."

They turned onto her street. She could see the house ahead.

"This is good," she said.

Jake slowed to a stop. She slid off the handlebars, landing harder than she meant to, catching herself on his arm.

"Graceful," he said.

"Always."

Her phone buzzed. Lily: *omg you missed EVERYTHING. Ethan's dad showed up. huge fight. everyone's still weird.*

Sophie stared at the screen. Another text: *where are you??*

"Everything okay?" Jake was watching her.

"Drama at the house." She looked toward the front door. "I'm not ready to go in yet."

Jake glanced at the house then back at her. "Beach?"

They left the bike in the driveway and headed down to the beach. It was empty this late, just the black shape of the water and the stars coming out overhead. They found a spot past the high-tide line and sat.

"So what happened?" he asked.

"I don't know yet. Something with Ethan's dad. His parents are divorced." She pulled her knees up. "Half the people in that house are divorced or getting divorced. It's like a support group that accidentally rented a beach house."

Jake grinned. "That bad?"

"No. I mean, they're good. They're my mom's best friends. I've known all of them my whole life." She dug her fingers into the cool sand. "It's just a lot sometimes. Everyone dealing with their stuff, and I'm supposed to be the easy one. The one who doesn't need anything."

"Are you fine?"

She didn't answer right away. The waves kept coming in.

"You know I have a boyfriend," she said. "Trevor."

"You mentioned."

"He's great. He's—" She stopped. "I don't know why I'm telling you this."

"Because I'm here and you wanted to." Jake leaned back on his hands. "Also, I'm very easy to talk to. It's a gift."

She laughed. "Trevor's great, but I'm leaving for college in the fall. And he's got another year of high school. And I keep thinking—" She shook her head. "Never mind."

"You keep thinking it's already over, you just haven't said it yet."

Sophie looked at him. He was watching the water, not her.

"My parents were like that," he said. "Knew it was done for years before they actually said it. They stayed together until my sister graduated, then sat us down like it was some big announcement. But we already knew." He shrugged. "I was relieved, honestly. But it also sucked. Both things at once."

"Both things at once," Sophie repeated.

"Yeah."

Neither of them spoke for a while. Down the beach, someone was walking a dog, a flashlight beam bouncing along the waterline.

"I don't know what I feel," Sophie said finally. "About Trevor. About any of it. Everyone else seems to know when something's over. And I'm just... here. Waiting to figure it out."

"Maybe that's okay," Jake said. "Maybe you don't have to know yet."

"Maybe."

He stood and brushed the sand off his shorts, then held out a hand. She took it, let him pull her up.

"You seem like you're handling things," he said. "Even if you don't feel like it."

"Thanks."

They walked back toward the street, the house bright against the dark. At the bike, Jake stopped.

His hand brushed her arm as he reached for the handlebars. Maybe an accident. Maybe not.

He pushed off, pedaling back the way they'd come, and Sophie stood on the sidewalk until he disappeared around the corner.

Then she went inside to find out what Lily meant by *huge fight*.

* * *

Later, after dinner had been cleaned up and the house had dispersed into its separate corners, Meredith found Tom on the rooftop.

He was sitting in one of the teak lounge chairs, beer in hand, looking out at the dark ocean. She sat down beside him with her own glass of wine.

"What a day," she said.

"It was."

They sat in silence for a moment. Then Meredith said, "I've been thinking. About the retirement plan."

Tom took a sip of his beer but didn't respond. Waiting.

"I can't walk away from the practice. Not yet." She looked at her wine rather than at him. "I know you've been running numbers, and I know the math works. But I've spent fifteen years building something, and I'm not done."

"I never said you had to sell."

"You said 'we.' You said if we sold, we'd never have to work again."

Tom set down his beer. "That was a possibility. Not a plan."

"It sounded like a plan."

Tom turned to look at her. "Meredith. I've known you for twenty-four years. Do you really think I expected you to agree without discussing it? I was starting a conversation. That's all."

She didn't answer. The wine was cool in her hand, the glass sweating slightly in the evening air.

"What do you want?" he asked.

"I'm still working through it."

"Then take your time. I can wait."

"What if I figure out something you don't like?" She finally looked at him.

"Then we talk about it. That's what we do."

She set her glass on the deck and got up from her chair, crossed to his, and settled onto his lap. His arms came around her automatically. She draped hers around his neck.

"We're okay?" she asked.

"We're always okay."

She kissed him.

After the day they'd had, after everything—she could still do this. They could still do this.

CHAPTER TEN

The sectional was more comfortable than Jen had expected, which was good, since she'd been sleeping on it for over a week now. Tom's surprise arrival had bumped her from Meredith's room, and nobody had figured out a better arrangement since.

She lay there in the dim room, staring at the ceiling, listening to the house. Nothing stirred. Even the ocean seemed quieter at this hour, the waves a distant murmur rather than their usual insistence. The sliding doors reflected the interior back at her, the beach beyond them still invisible.

She'd finished it.

She kept waiting for that to feel different. Last night, sometime after eleven, she'd typed the last sentence of the Clementine Fields draft. Not a triumphant final line, not some perfectly crafted resolution that wrapped everything up in a bow. Just Clementine standing in the doorway of her bookshop, watching the rain fall on Brambleton's cobblestones, knowing that some mysteries stayed solved and some didn't, and that was the nature of things.

Jen had sat there in the dark afterward, laptop still open, the cursor blinking at the end of the document. She'd waited for relief. For celebration. For something to mark the moment.

What she'd felt instead was emptiness. The kind that came when something you'd been gripping finally slipped away. Not lost, just finished. And your hands were free.

She sat up slowly. The floor was cool under her feet. She found her phone wedged between the cushions and checked the time: 5:47. Early. But her brain was already running, and she knew sleep wasn't coming back.

She pulled on a cardigan over her tank top and padded to the kitchen, moving quietly so she wouldn't wake anyone. Slid a pod into the Keurig and waited while it hissed and sputtered through its cycle. She leaned against the counter, watching the coffee fill her mug.

Three hundred and twelve pages. Six murders, one nosy protagonist, and a resolution that her editor would probably love. She'd send it today. Or tomorrow. Whenever she worked up the nerve to let it go.

The fantasy romance was still there too, sitting in a separate folder on her desktop, growing every time she looked away from the mystery. Over sixty pages now. She'd given her heroine a ruined kingdom to rebuild and a grief she couldn't outrun, and at some point the story had stopped feeling like an escape and started feeling like a confession. It wasn't what she was supposed to be writing. It also wouldn't leave her alone.

When the Keurig finished, she took her mug out to the deck off the living room, settling into one of the chairs facing the ocean.

The sun was already up, low and bright over the water. The beach was empty except for a man with a metal detector working his way along the tide line, headphones on, lost in whatever signals the sand was sending him.

Jen wrapped both hands around her mug and watched the light shift and settle.

The sliding door opened behind her.

"You're up early." Meredith appeared with her own mug,

hair still mussed from sleep, wearing the oversized Penn State shirt she'd stolen from Tom years ago.

"Couldn't sleep."

Meredith sank into the chair beside her. Neither of them said anything. The man with the detector had moved farther down the beach, a small figure against the morning light.

"You finished the book," Meredith said. Not a question.

"How did you know?"

"You're up before six, you're not writing, and you haven't checked your phone once." She held her mug closer. "Last night?"

"Around eleven."

"Why didn't you say something?"

"Everyone was already in bed. And—" Jen took a sip of coffee. "It didn't feel like a celebration moment. It felt like a holding-my-breath moment."

"What are you holding your breath for?"

"That's just it—I don't know." She laughed, but it came out strange. "I was so focused on finishing, I never thought about what happens after. Now it's done, and I have no idea what comes next."

Meredith paused. "Isn't that what comes next? The not-knowing?"

"You're very philosophical for six in the morning."

"I'm working on it." Meredith lifted her mug.

They sat together as the light strengthened. A jogger appeared, running along the hard sand near the water.

"I've been writing something else," Jen said. "On the side. Not Clementine."

Meredith turned to look at her.

"Fantasy romance. Completely off-brand. My editor would have a stroke." Jen stared into her mug. "But I can't stop. The heroine's angry in a way Clementine never gets to be, and I think that's why I keep going back to it."

"Is it good?"

"I'm not sure. It feels different. Like the words are coming from somewhere I haven't accessed in a while." She watched the jogger disappear past the jetty. "There's this guy I met at the coffee shop. Clint. He's a musician, plays guitar. We've been talking about the creative stuff, the blocks, the doubt, all of it. He thinks I should keep going with the fantasy."

"A guy at a coffee shop." Meredith's eyebrows rose. "And you're just mentioning this now?"

"It's not like that. He's just—he gets it. The thing where you're supposed to be making one thing but you can't stop making something else." She set her mug on the arm of the chair. "He invited me to his show. Thursday night at the Hard Rock."

"Are you going to go?" Meredith asked.

"Maybe." Jen shrugged.

Meredith smiled, but it was knowing rather than teasing. "You know you're going."

"I really don't."

She looked out at the water instead of at Meredith. The man with the detector was heading back the other way now, sweeping in slow arcs.

"It's been a long time since I let myself want something without knowing how it would turn out," Jen said finally. "The book, the fantasy, all of it. I've spent so long writing the safe thing, saying the safe thing, staying in my lane."

"And now?" Meredith watched her.

"Now the book is done. And I'm still here. And maybe it's time to stop waiting for certainty before I do anything."

* * *

The morning unfolded in the usual chaos.

By nine, the house was awake and loud. Coffee mugs accumulated in the sink. Someone was hunting for sunscreen. Someone else was arguing about whose turn it was to make the Wawa run. The teenagers had emerged in stages, Max first with his hair standing up in three directions, then Lily still half-asleep and looking for her phone.

"Has anyone seen my phone?" Lily asked, for the third time.

"You're holding it," Max said.

Lily looked at her hand. She was, in fact, holding her phone. "I hate you."

"Love you too."

Sophie and Brittany came down together, already dressed, talking about the beach club and free smoothies. Ethan wandered through, looking more relaxed than he had in days, and actually said good morning to Lori before grabbing a banana and heading for the deck.

"Mark the calendar," Carrie murmured.

"Don't jinx it," Lori said, but she was smiling.

Jen had showered and changed by then, restless in a way that coffee hadn't fixed. She needed to move. Needed to be somewhere that wasn't the house, a place to think without the comfortable noise of eleven people living on top of each other.

"I'm going for a walk," she announced to whoever was listening. "Might be a while."

Carrie looked up from the fruit she was cutting. "You okay?"

"Better than okay. Just need some air."

She headed out before the questions started.

The promenade was already busy with the morning crowd: families hauling wagons toward the beach, couples on bikes, a group of older women power-walking in matching visors. Jen walked against the flow, heading south toward Landis, past the ice cream shops that hadn't opened yet and the surf rental places setting out their boards.

She didn't have a destination. That was the point.

The streets off the promenade were quieter, residential blocks mixed with the occasional shop. She passed a yoga studio with a class in progress, bodies visible through the window, moving in unison, then a florist arranging buckets outside. Birds of paradise, sunflowers, purple hydrangeas.

Wax & Water sat on Pleasure Avenue near 40th, tucked between a surf shop and a place that sold nothing but wind chimes. She'd walked past it at least a dozen times since they'd arrived but had never gone in. The kind of place you noticed without entering, if you noticed record stores at all.

Today, she pushed open the door.

Inside, it smelled like dust and vinyl and something faintly sweet. Aged wood, maybe, or incense from a decade ago that had never quite faded. The shop was smaller than it looked from outside, narrow and deep. Bins of records ran along both walls, and stacks of CDs and cassettes took up the back corner. Concert posters covered every available surface, layered on top of each other, dates from the '80s and '90s and some so faded you couldn't read them anymore. Behind the counter, an older man with bleached-blond hair and thick black-framed glasses sorted through a box of vinyl without looking up. Old tattoos on his forearms, a Ramones shirt that had seen better decades.

Jen moved to the nearest bin and started browsing.

She hadn't bought a record in years. But the ritual appealed. The tactile satisfaction of flipping through album covers, seeing artwork that had been designed to be held in your hands rather than scrolled past on a screen.

The bins were organized by some personal logic she couldn't decode. She moved through rock, then jazz, then what seemed to be entirely live albums from bands she'd never heard of.

She was near the back, pulling out a Beastie Boys album she hadn't listened to since college, when she heard footsteps on stairs. A door half-hidden behind some crates swung open, and Clint emerged from what looked like a basement, a stack of records tucked under his arm.

He stopped when he saw her.

"Are you following me?" she asked, but she was smiling.

"I was here first." He nodded toward the stairs. "Buddy lets me dig through the back stock before he puts it out. Standing arrangement."

He was wearing an old T-shirt that might have once been black, and jeans worn soft at the knees. He looked like he'd been up for hours, which probably meant he'd just gotten out of bed.

"You're down here at—" She glanced at her phone. "Nine in the morning, digging through a basement?"

"Best stuff goes fast. You snooze, you lose." He shifted the records. "What about you? Didn't take you for a vinyl person."

"I'm not. Or I wasn't." She looked down at the album in her hands.

"Paul's Boutique." He tilted his head approvingly. "Good choice. Most people go for Licensed to Ill, but this one's the real gem."

"I finished the book last night," she said, not sure why she was telling him.

"Which one?" Clint leaned against the bin.

"The mystery." She shook her head. "Woke up this morning not knowing what to do with myself."

Clint set his records on top of the bin beside her. "That sounds about right."

"Does it?" Her eyebrows rose.

"When you've been working on something that long, it becomes part of how you think. Then it's done and you have all this space where it used to be." He stepped closer, eyes on the bin rather than on her. "After we finished our last album, I kept waking up in the middle of the night thinking I should be at the studio."

"How'd you get past it?" Jen asked.

"Started writing new stuff. Different stuff." He glanced at her. "That fantasy you mentioned. The off-brand one. You still working on it?"

"It's grown. A lot." Jen straightened slightly.

"Good." Clint nodded. "That's how you know it's real."

She slid the Beastie Boys album back into the bin then pulled it out again. "Last time we talked, you said I already knew what I wanted to do. That I was just afraid."

"Sounds like something I'd say." He smiled, just slightly.

"You were right. I knew. I just couldn't admit it while the mystery was still hanging over me." She flipped the album to read the track listing. "But I finished it. And I don't have that excuse anymore."

"So what's next?" His voice was gentle.

"That's the terrifying part." Jen exhaled. "I don't know."

"Also the good part." He shifted his grip on the records. "Hey. Thursday. The residency. You should come."

Her head lifted. "Yeah?"

"The new stuff I mentioned? It's been landing. Thursdays especially. The crowd's different, more listening than dancing." He looked almost shy. "I'd like you to hear it. If you want."

"The Hard Rock's not exactly around the corner," Jen pointed out.

"Forty minutes." He shrugged. "Less if you hit the lights right."

"Okay," she said.

"Okay?" Clint looked surprised.

"I'll come. Thursday."

His smile this time was slower, more careful. "I'll leave your name at the door."

"You don't have to do that," she said.

"I want to." He hesitated. "Jen. The fantasy book. Whatever it is, wherever it goes, keep writing it. The thing you're not supposed to be making is usually what matters most."

He walked toward the counter without waiting for a

response. She watched him go, saw him set down his stack and start talking to the owner, gesturing at one of the albums, falling into what was clearly a familiar argument about condition and value.

She carried the album to the register.

The guy looked up when she approached, gave a small nod to Clint, and rang her up without comment. Nine dollars. She paid in cash, and he slid the record into a brown paper bag with a logo she didn't recognize.

"Good album," the guy said, and it sounded like it physically pained him to offer a compliment.

"Thanks."

"Don't play it on anything cheap." He handed her the bag like he was entrusting her with a family heirloom. "You'll ruin it."

"I'm not even sure I still have a turntable."

He stared at her. Clint, behind her, made a sound that might have been a laugh.

"Then why are you buying it?" the guy asked.

"I have no idea," Jen said honestly, and walked out before he could take it back.

* * *

Olivia stopped walking when she saw the nail salon.

She'd been up all night, Lily's words playing on a loop. They kissed. For a long time. Dan outside their house at two in the morning. Rachel in her car. Everything he'd sworn hadn't happened, happening. Eventually the house had woken up around her, and she'd slipped out the door without saying goodbye to anyone.

Now she was here. A place called Polished, its windows lined with neon-pink cursive and photos of manicured hands. The sign said WALK-INS WELCOME.

She went inside.

The woman at the front glanced over. "Good morning. Walk-in?"

"Yes." Her voice sounded strange to her own ears. Flat. "Mani-pedi."

They led her to one of the massage chairs along the wall, the kind with the built-in footbath. Olivia leaned back into it and let the water run warm over her feet while someone started on her hands at the little table beside her. Two women working at once, efficient and focused, not interested in small talk. She stared at the TV above her, some home renovation show with the sound off, and let her mind go blank.

She wasn't okay. Wouldn't be okay for a while.

But she was clear. That was what surprised her. After months of confusion, of trying to decide if she could forgive him, of weighing what was fair and what was possible, she'd finally arrived somewhere solid.

"Color?"

Olivia blinked. The woman doing her feet was waiting, gesturing at the wall of polish.

She scanned the rows of bottles without really seeing them. Pinks, reds, neutrals. All the safe choices she'd been making for years. Then her eyes landed on a bottle in the corner.

A bright blue. Electric, almost cobalt. She'd picked it up once at a salon back home, and Dan had made a face. *That's a little much, isn't it?* She'd put it back and gotten the pale pink instead.

"That one," she said. "Same for both."

When her feet were done, they moved her to a table to finish drying her toes and complete the manicure. She sat there watching the blue go on her fingernails, one hand and then the other, while couples walked past the window outside and the renovation show played silently above her.

Outside, twenty minutes later, she stood on the sidewalk with her nails still tacky and her phone in her hand. She didn't remember pulling it out.

Olivia dialed Dan's number.

He answered on the second ring, cheerful and oblivious. "Hey, babe. I was just thinking about you. How's the trip going?"

Olivia let him talk. Let him ask about the weather, the house, whether the kids were having fun. He sounded normal. Sounded like the man she'd been married to for seventeen years, the father of her children, the person she was supposed to be saving this marriage for.

"Lily told me something the other night," she said when he'd run out of pleasantries.

A pause. "What?"

"She saw you. In January. Outside the house." Olivia's voice was steady, steadier than she felt. "With Rachel. At two in the morning."

The silence stretched. She could hear him breathing, could almost see him on the other end of the line, trying to figure out what to say. What story to tell.

"Olivia, it wasn't—"

"Don't." The word came out sharper than she intended. "Don't tell me it wasn't what I think. Don't tell me I misunderstood. Our daughter saw you kiss another woman outside our house in the middle of the night. She's been carrying that for five months because she was scared to tell me. She's fifteen years old, and she's been keeping your secret because she was afraid of what would happen if she didn't."

"I was going to tell you. I just—" His voice cracked.

"You looked me in the eye. In the counselor's office. You swore it was only emotional. That nothing physical happened." Her eyes closed. "And I believed you. That's on me. But the lying—that's on you."

"It was only once," Dan said. "It didn't mean anything."

"It meant everything." She waited for her voice to shake. It didn't. "I've spent six months trying to forgive you for something you told me was just texts. Just feelings. Just a mistake that didn't actually cross any lines. And the whole time, you were lying."

"Olivia, please. We can work through this. We can—"

"No." The word was soft but final. "We can't."

"You can't just decide that on a phone call." She could hear him pacing. "We should talk about this, face to face, when you get back—"

"I'm done, Dan." She heard herself say it and knew she meant it. "Not done talking. Not done for now. Done. I can't keep trying to save something you already broke."

"The counseling, the effort, doesn't that count for anything?"

"It might have," Olivia said. "If you'd told me the truth."

He didn't answer. Traffic hummed faintly on his end, the familiar silence of the house she'd left behind.

"The kids—" he started.

"The kids will be fine. They're strong, and they have both of us, and they'll be fine." She exhaled. "I'll call you when I get back. We can figure out logistics then."

"Olivia, wait—"

She hung up.

The phone stayed in her hand, screen going dark. Seventeen years, ending outside a nail salon in Sea Isle City. She braced for the collapse, the tears. They didn't come.

Instead, she felt still. The noise in her head—the arguments, the justifications, the endless calculations—had simply stopped.

Olivia started walking. No direction, just motion. Past houses with their beach chairs stacked on porches, past kids on bikes, past a dog-walking service with four leashes tangled together. The town moved around her, oblivious to the fact that her marriage had just ended in under five minutes.

Her phone buzzed once, twice, three times. She didn't look.

After a while, she made her way back toward the house. The shape of it rising against the sky, already starting to feel like theirs. Someone was on the rooftop deck. Voices drifted up from the pool.

The blue polish was perfect. Bright and unapologetic. The kind of thing Dan would have called "a little much." She smiled at her hands and kept walking.

CHAPTER ELEVEN

Lori had been to the vineyard once before, for the barrier islands talk John had hosted, but that had been a quieter affair. Thirty people in folding chairs, an academic at the podium, the sort of event where you took notes if you were that sort of person. Tonight was different.

Long wooden tables had replaced the chairs, lined with wine glasses and small plates of cheese and crackers. The crowd was twice the size and twice as loud, people standing three deep near the bar, conversation spilling out past the flag-stone patio and into the vineyard rows. Someone had set out mason jars stuffed with wildflowers as centerpieces, and the globe lights strung along the patio glowed brighter against the darker sky.

The vineyard stretched out beyond the gathering, rows of trellised vines catching the last of the daylight. The barn doors were propped open, revealing more seating inside and a makeshift stage where a microphone stood waiting. People milled around with glasses of red and white, their voices blending into the low hum of a crowd that didn't know yet what kind of night they were in for.

Lori found a spot near the back of the patio, close enough

to see the stage but far enough that she could slip away if she needed to. She wasn't sure why she'd come, except that John had mentioned it. Captain Ron Bosco, a fisherman who'd written a memoir nobody expected to be good. She'd said she'd be there, and now here she was.

She ordered a glass of the house white from a woman working a folding table near the barn entrance. The wine was better than she'd expected, crisp with a hint of pear underneath. She took a sip and let herself look around.

John was near the stage, talking to a man who had to be Captain Ron. Even from across the crowd, Lori could see the captain was everything the description had promised: seventies, maybe older, with skin the color of old leather and hands that looked like they'd hauled nets in every kind of weather. He wore a button-down shirt that might have been dress clothes by his standards, the sleeves rolled up to reveal forearms roped with muscle and marked with faded tattoos. His white hair was cropped short, and when he laughed at something John said, his whole face creased into it.

John said something else, gestured toward the crowd that was still filling in. Ron nodded then clapped him on the shoulder with one of those rough hands. They both turned to look out at the gathering audience, and for a second, John's eyes swept the patio.

They landed on her.

He smiled—not the professional host smile she'd seen him give other people, but smaller, more genuine. He lifted his hand in a half-wave, then turned back to Ron.

Lori's pulse skipped.

She took a seat at one of the long tables, nodding to the couple beside her, sixties, regulars who looked like they attended every event the vineyard put on. More people filtered in over the next fifteen minutes. The seats filled. Someone dimmed the lights slightly, focusing attention toward the stage.

John stepped to the microphone.

"Thanks for coming out tonight," he said, and the chatter died down. He gave his usual opening, the bookstore, the series, his frustration with traditional author events, and Lori smiled at lines she'd heard before. The crowd laughed in the right places. A few newcomers leaned in, curious. But she was watching John, the way he warmed to an audience, the ease that came over him when he talked about something he loved.

He gestured toward Ron, who was standing off to the side with his arms crossed, looking vaguely uncomfortable with the attention.

"Tonight's guest doesn't need much introduction, but I'm going to give him one anyway because he'd never do it himself. Captain Ron Bosco has been fishing these waters for fifty years. Fifty years. He's survived hurricanes, engine failures, a whale that nearly capsized his boat, and three ex-wives—" Ron made a sound that was half-laugh, half-protest. "He wrote a memoir last year. Self-published it himself because no publisher would touch it. Said it was too raw. Too honest. Not enough plot." John paused. "I read it in one sitting and called him the next day. Told him it was the best book about the sea I'd read in twenty years. He told me I was full of it. But he agreed to come talk to you anyway."

He stepped aside, and Ron took the microphone with the reluctance of a man who'd rather be anywhere else.

"I don't know why any of you are here," Ron said, his voice carrying easily without amplification. "It's a beautiful evening. You could be at the beach. You could be at a bar. Instead you're listening to an old man talk about fish."

He looked around the crowd, squinting slightly like he was trying to figure out what he was dealing with.

"All right, then. Let's get into it."

He didn't read from his book. He didn't need to. The stories came out like he was sitting at a bar with friends, like he'd told them a hundred times before and never got tired of the telling. The first time he went out on a commercial boat, sixteen years old and terrified, throwing up over the rail for the first three hours while the crew pretended not to notice. Learning to read the weather, the water, the way the birds moved when something was about to change. The old-timers who'd taught him everything and were gone now, every one of them, their names forgotten by everyone except him.

"The sea doesn't care about you," Ron said, maybe twenty minutes in. "That's the first thing you learn. It's not mean. It's not kind. It just is. You can respect it, you can learn its moods, you can do everything right, and it can still kill you. That's the deal. You accept the deal, or you stay on shore."

He told the storm story. October of '91, a nor'easter that came in faster than anyone predicted. Ron had been running for port with a crew of four, watching the barometer drop like it was falling off a cliff. He'd made a decision, push through or wait it out, and he'd chosen wrong. The next six hours were the longest of his life. Waves that came over the bow like walls of gray-green water. The engine choking, then catching, then choking again. Two of his crew lashed to the rails because there was nothing else to hold onto.

"We made it," he said. "Obviously. I'm standing here. But I still dream about that storm sometimes. Wake up thinking I can hear the water coming."

The crowd had gone completely still. Lori leaned forward.

Ron shifted, took a sip from the water glass someone had set on the table beside him. When he spoke again, his voice was lighter.

"But it's not all terror and near-death experiences. Sometimes the sea gives you something back."

He told the whale story. A morning run, nothing special, a day you wouldn't remember afterward. They'd been hauling in nets when a shape surfaced beside the boat. Not a splash. A presence. A humpback, maybe forty feet long, rising slowly like it had all the time in the world. It came up so close the hull scraped against its side. Ron could have reached out and touched it.

"I thought we were dead," he said. "Thought it was going to roll us over and that would be it. But it just—looked at me. Eye the size of a grapefruit, looking right into mine. And then it sank back down, slow as it came up, and disappeared."

He paused.

"I've been out there fifty years. Seen a lot of things I can't explain. But that's the one I think about most. That whale chose to come up beside us. Chose to let us see it. And then it left. Like it was saying hello, or goodbye, or both."

The crowd exhaled together.

She glanced across the patio. John was leaning against the barn doorframe, arms crossed, watching Ron with an expression she couldn't read. Pride, maybe. Affection.

Then his eyes shifted and found hers again.

This time, neither of them looked away.

Ron kept going. The story about the net that pulled up a creature none of them could identify. He wouldn't say what exactly, just that they threw it back and never talked about it after. The way he said it made everyone laugh, even as a chill ran down Lori's spine. Then the story about his first mate who went overboard in rough seas, how Ron had jumped in after him without thinking and held onto him for forty minutes until the boat could circle back. When he told that one, his voice caught, and he had to pause, looking down at his hands.

"Sorry," he said. "That one still gets me."

The crowd waited. Someone near the front wiped their eyes.

"His name was Bud Casper," Ron said. "Good man. Stubborn as an anchor. He passed about five years ago. His heart gave out, not the sea, which would have made him laugh. But I still think about those forty minutes. Holding onto him in that water, both of us sure we were going to die. You learn things about a person in forty minutes like that. Things you can't learn any other way."

He told a few more stories after that, but the mood had shifted. Lighter ones, funnier ones. The running joke about his second ex-wife and the nor'easter that hit the same week she served him papers. "I'll tell you which one caused more damage, but I don't want to get sued." The whole room lost it at that one. Someone actually snorted wine.

Then the Q&A. The usual questions at first. How did he get started, what was his favorite boat, did he have any advice for young fishermen. Ron answered them all with the same gruff honesty, dismissing the sentimental ones, leaning into the practical.

Near the end, a woman in the front row raised her hand.

"Captain Bosco, after all this time on the water, what keeps you going back?"

Ron was quiet. The patio hushed, even the breeze dying down. Someone coughed.

"You want the real answer?" he asked.

"Yes."

He looked out at the crowd, and his expression changed. Less performer, more the man underneath.

"The sea's the only place I ever felt like myself," he said. "Everything on land, the marriages, the money problems, the ways I've let people down, it all goes quiet out there. It's just me and the water and whatever's going to happen that day. And I know that sounds like I'm running away from something. Maybe I am. But it's also where I run to. Where I've always run to." He shrugged. "That's the best I can do. I hope it's enough of an answer."

The woman nodded. The crowd applauded. John stepped forward to close things out, thanking Ron, reminding everyone that copies of the memoir were available at the table near the barn and that Ron would be happy to sign them, though Ron's expression suggested "happy" was a strong word.

People started to move. Chairs scraped back. The energy changed, audience becoming mingling crowd. Lori stayed where she was, watching people stream toward the signing table, the wine, each other.

The couple beside her stood up and headed for refills. Lori thought about doing the same, then thought about slipping out before the crowd thinned enough to make her visible.

Then John appeared at the end of her table.

"What did you think?" he asked, sliding into the empty seat beside her.

"I think I need to buy that book."

"I have a copy in my car. Consider it a gift."

"You don't have to—"

"I want to." He smiled. "Ron would give them away for free if I let him. Says he didn't write it to make money. He wrote it because the stories needed to go somewhere before he forgot them."

Lori glanced over at Ron, who was shaking hands with someone. "He's something."

"He's the real thing. You don't find that very often."

The crowd was thinning now. People drifting off to their cars, to the last glasses of wine, to whatever came next. The globe lights grew warmer as the sky darkened.

"I should let you—" Lori started, gesturing vaguely toward the cleanup that was beginning to happen around them.

"Stay," John said. "If you want. The vineyard doesn't close for another hour, and I could use the company."

"Okay."

They moved to a table at the edge of the patio, the one farthest from the cleanup crew now stacking chairs and collecting glasses. John brought a bottle of red and poured them each a glass. The last of the audience members had either left or were clustered around Ron, who was still signing books with the air of a man serving a sentence.

"He hates this part," John said, following her gaze. "The talking-to-strangers part. He'd rather be on a boat."

"Then why does he do it?"

"Because I asked him to. And because somewhere in that crusty exterior, he actually wants people to read what he wrote. He just can't admit it."

The wine was different from what she'd been drinking earlier. Darker, fuller, a red that made you slow down. Lori took a sip and settled in.

"How did you find him?" she asked. "The book, I mean."

"Estate sale, if you can believe it. A woman in Avalon passed away, and her family was selling off her library. I bought three boxes of books without looking too closely. Ron's memoir was buried at the bottom of one of them." He shook his head. "No idea how it ended up there. She must have bought it at one of the craft fairs where he was selling copies out of a cooler. But I took it home, started reading, and couldn't stop."

"And you just—called him?"

"His number was in the back of the book. Self-published, remember. He put his personal phone number in the author bio like it was nothing." John laughed. "He answered on the second ring and asked if I was trying to sell him something. When I told him I wanted to host a reading, he was quiet for so long I thought he'd hung up. Then he said, 'You're serious?' And I said, 'Completely.' And he said, 'Well, I'll be.' And that was that."

Across the patio, Ron was finally free of the signing line. He caught John's eye, raised a hand in farewell, and headed toward the parking lot without looking back.

"He's not coming over to say goodbye?" Lori asked.

"Ron doesn't do goodbyes. He just leaves." John watched him go. "We've been fishing together a few times since I found that book. He barely talks, but I feel like I've known him for years."

"I think I like him."

"Most people do, once they get past the gruffness." John reached for the bottle. "More?"

"Better not. I'm driving."

"Probably wise. Unlike hiding behind your friend at Ocean Drive."

Lori groaned. "You saw that."

"Hard to miss." He was grinning. "For what it's worth, my sister thought it was charming. She also told me I should ask you out, but that felt like something a teenager would do."

"And yet here we are."

"Here we are."

He topped off his own glass and set the bottle aside. "You mentioned friends, kids, a summer rental, but that's the brochure version. What's the real reason you're here?"

She'd been giving the brochure version since June. The rental house, the friends, the kids. The easy answer that fit into small talk.

"Honestly?" She turned her wine glass in her hands. "I'm figuring some things out."

"What kind of things?"

The safe version was on her tongue again. But John was looking at her with that focused attention she'd noticed the first time they'd talked, like he actually wanted to hear the answer, not just fill the silence.

"My marriage ended three years ago," she said. "My ex-husband is getting remarried in a few weeks. To someone who was—around—before things ended. My son is seventeen and angry about all of it, and I'm trying to help him without making it worse. Some days I feel like I'm finally figuring out who I actually am. Other days I feel like I'm just pretending until the next thing falls apart."

The words came out faster than she'd intended. She took a breath.

"Sorry. That was more than you asked for."

"No," John said. "That was exactly what I asked for."

The staff had moved inside now, their voices muffled through the barn doors. The patio was nearly empty except for the two of them, the vineyard stretching dark beyond the tables.

"I understand the figuring-things-out part," John said. "I was married for eighteen years. Divorced for almost ten now. It took me a long time to stop defining myself by the failure of it."

"When did that change?"

"I told you I burned out on corporate life. But I didn't tell you the moment I knew." He traced the rim of his glass with one finger. "I was sitting in a meeting about quarterly projections, and I realized I couldn't remember the last time I'd read a book for pleasure. The last time I'd done anything just because I wanted to. That was the day I started planning my exit."

"And everyone thought you were crazy."

"My ex-wife called to tell me I was making a mistake. My kids thought I'd lost my mind." He shrugged. "They've come around. My daughter brought her husband down last summer and spent the whole weekend browsing the shelves and telling me she was proud of me. My son still thinks I should have kept the consulting job, but he also asks for book recommendations now, so I count that as progress."

Someone inside the barn turned off a light, and the patio grew dimmer. The stars were visible now, scattered across the sky in a way they never were back home.

"Can I ask you something?" John said.

"Sure."

"Why did you come tonight? I mean, I'm glad you did. But you could have stayed home, or with your friends. You could have been anywhere."

Lori met his eyes. "Because you invited me," she said. "And I wanted to see you again."

John was quiet. The patio had emptied around them. A breeze stirred the vines.

Then he stood up.

"Come with me," he said.

He led her past the last of the tables, to where a low stone wall separated the flagstones from the vineyard beyond. They walked along the wall for a few yards until they reached a gap, a pathway between the rows of vines.

"The owners don't mind if you walk through," John said. "I've done it a hundred times."

They moved into the vineyard, the vines rising on either side, the leaves rustling softly in the breeze. The path was narrow enough that they had to walk close together. Lori was aware of his shoulder near hers, the sound of his footsteps on the packed earth.

They emerged on the other side into a small clearing, a bench overlooking a pond she hadn't known was there. The water reflected the stars, doubled and scattered across its surface. Fireflies blinked in the grass along the edges.

"I come here sometimes," John said. "When I need to think. Or when I need to stop thinking."

They sat on the bench. The night sounds surrounded them. Crickets, the distant hum of the highway, a bullfrog somewhere near the water.

"I need to say something," John said. "Before I lose my nerve."

Lori looked at him. The starlight caught the silver in his hair, the lines around his eyes, how he was watching her—nervous and hopeful and trying not to show either one.

"I've been thinking about you," he said. "More than I probably should."

"How long?"

"Since the first time you came into the store." His mouth

quirked. "You asked for a recommendation and I could tell you actually meant it. You weren't just making conversation. You wanted to find something real."

"That's what you noticed?"

"I remember everything about that conversation." He shook his head. "That's not—I don't usually—I'm not doing this well."

Lori laughed. The sound surprised her, easy and unguarded.

"You're doing fine," she said.

Behind them, back toward the barn, someone called John's name. Distant, probably one of the staff wondering where he'd gone.

Neither made any move to go.

"They're going to come looking for you," Lori said.

"Let them."

The frog by the pond went quiet. The fireflies kept blinking.

She looked at him, and then she leaned in and kissed him.

It was soft at first, tentative—a question more than a statement. His hand came up to cup her face, gentle, like she might pull away. She didn't.

When they pulled apart, they were both breathing differently. Even the highway seemed farther away.

"Well," John said.

"Well," Lori agreed. She was smiling and couldn't seem to stop.

Someone called his name again, closer this time.

"I should go deal with that," he said, but he didn't move.

"You should."

He reached for her hand, squeezed it once. Then Lori laughed again—that same easy sound—and rose from the bench. "Go. I'll find my way back."

"I'll see you soon," he said.

"I'm not hard to find."

He smiled. The full version this time, not held back. Then he headed toward the voice, glancing over his shoulder once before disappearing between the vines.

Lori sat back down on the bench. The pond held the sky's reflection, patient and still. She wasn't ready to leave. Not yet.

* * *

Brittany had never been kayaking before. Not really, not the kind where you actually paddled somewhere instead of just drifting around a calm lake. But Ryan had suggested it after their shift, said he knew a spot, and she'd said yes before she could overthink it.

Now they were here, sliding through the back bay in rented kayaks, the sun dropping toward the mainland and turning everything gold. The beach club felt like it belonged to a different world. Out here, there was just the water and the marsh grass and the sound of their paddles dipping in and out.

"You're doing good," Ryan said from his kayak, a few feet ahead of hers. "Most first-timers tip over by now."

"Is that supposed to be encouraging?"

"Take the win."

She adjusted her grip on the paddle, trying to find the rhythm he'd shown her. Dip, pull, lift, switch sides. Her arms were already starting to ache, but she didn't want to say anything. The water here was shallow enough that she could see the bottom in some places, sandy and scattered with shells and the occasional dark shape of something alive.

Ryan guided them toward a channel between two stretches of marsh. The grass rose on either side, taller than she'd expected, dense and green, wild and orderly at once.

"My grandfather used to bring me through here when I was a kid," Ryan said, his paddle resting across his kayak. "Before the crabbing, before anything else. He'd cut the motor

164

and just let us drift." He nodded at the grass. "Said you had to listen to a place before you could understand it."

"What did you hear?"

He was quiet, tilting his head like he was trying to remember. "Everything. How a mullet jumps and you can tell by the splash if it's running from something. The sound the water makes moving through the grass. Different than open bay, softer." He slowed his paddling, letting her catch up. "He knew this marsh the way some people know their own house. Could tell you where the blues would be running just by the smell of the air."

They moved deeper into the marsh, the channel narrowing. The sounds changed. Less splashing, more birdsong, the soft rustle of wings somewhere overhead. A cormorant sat on a piling, wings spread to dry in the fading light.

"It's like nowhere else back here," Brittany said.

"That's what I love about it. The beach is great, but everyone sees the beach. This part—" He gestured at the marsh around them. "You have to want to find it."

They paddled in silence for a while. Brittany settled into the rhythm, the strokes, how the kayak responded to each movement, the calm that came when she stopped trying so hard.

"At the bonfire, you told me about your grandfather. The crabbing spots that don't work anymore." She paused, choosing her words. "Have you always wanted to protect this? Or did that come later?"

Ryan slowed his kayak, turning slightly so they were parallel. The sun was lower now, the light softer, catching the water in streaks of orange and pink.

"I think I always noticed things," he said. "But noticing isn't the same as doing something about it. For a long time I just figured someone else would handle it. Scientists, politicians, whoever." He dipped his paddle, let it drag through the water. "Then I took this marine biology class junior year. The professor brought in all these photos from the seventies. What the bay looked like back then. The seagrass beds, the oyster reefs. It was like a different planet. And I realized I couldn't just wait for someone else to handle it. If people like me didn't learn how this stuff worked, it would just keep getting worse."

Brittany watched his face as he talked. He wasn't looking at her. He was looking at the water, at the marsh, at the horizon beyond.

"So now you're out here every chance you get," she said. "Learning the names of things. Paying attention."

"Trying to." He ducked his head, almost embarrassed. "My family thinks I should be a doctor. Make real money. But I can't stop thinking about the water."

"That's—" She searched for the right word. "That's really beautiful, actually."

He glanced at her, surprised. "Most people think it's depressing."

"It's not depressing." She shook her head. "It's purposeful. Like you're not just drifting."

"That's exactly it."

They paddled on. The channel opened up into a wider stretch of water, the marsh falling away on one side to reveal a view of the bay and the distant shore beyond. The sun was almost touching the horizon now, the sky shifting through colors she didn't have names for.

"We should pull over here," Ryan said, pointing toward a small sandy bank. "Watch the sunset then head back. The current makes the return trip faster anyway."

They nosed the kayaks onto the sand and climbed out, pulling them up past the waterline. It was a tiny strip of beach, maybe twenty feet across, sheltered by the marsh grass on three sides. Hidden. Private.

Brittany sat down on the sand, wrapping her arms around her knees. Ryan sat beside her, close enough that she could feel the heat coming off his skin.

"Thanks for this," she said.

"Anytime."

The sun met the water and began to sink. A few birds flew past in silhouette, heading somewhere with purpose.

"I've been thinking," Ryan said, not looking at her. "About what you said the other night. At the bonfire."

"What did I say?"

"That you feel like everyone else knows what they want. What they're doing." He picked up a shell from the sand, turned it over in his hands. "I think that's just what it looks like from outside. Most people are making it up as they go."

"Even you?"

"Especially me." He kept turning the shell in his fingers. "I talk a good game about the environmental stuff because I've had time to think about it. But the rest of my life? Total mess. I'm working at a beach club instead of taking summer classes. I have no idea if the grad school thing will even work out."

"But you have a direction."

Ryan tossed the shell toward the water. It skipped once before sinking. "You don't need a plan at nineteen." He turned to look at her. "Look, I'm twenty-two and I'm still winging it."

"Tell that to everyone asking what I'm going to major in."

"Tell them to mind their own business." He smiled. "Or tell them you're exploring your options. That always sounds good."

She laughed. Only a sliver of orange remained above the horizon now.

"I didn't know it could feel like this," Brittany said. "Easy. Like I don't have to try so hard." She didn't look at him. "I keep waiting for something to go wrong, but it just—keeps being good."

"Maybe nothing's going to go wrong."

"Maybe." She let herself believe it.

She turned toward him. The last light was catching his face, softening the angles, and she forgot to be nervous.

"I like you," she said. "I wanted to say that out loud, even if it makes things weird."

Ryan didn't answer right away. He held her gaze, and she watched his expression shift—surprise, then a slow smile.

"It doesn't make things weird," he said.

Then he reached over and took her hand.

They sat like that as the sun finished setting, his hand warm around hers, not talking, the last glow fading around them. His thumb brushed across her knuckles, and her breath caught. She didn't want to move. Didn't want this moment to end.

When the first stars appeared, they were still holding on.

"We should head back," Brittany said eventually.

"Probably."

She stood and offered him her hand. He took it, let her pull him up, and held on a beat longer than necessary before releasing it.

They pushed the kayaks back into the water. The paddle back was easier, like Ryan had said, the current carrying them, the strokes coming naturally now. They didn't talk much, but the silence felt different than before. Fuller. Comfortable.

The launch spot came into view, the parking lot and the shore and the world they'd briefly left behind. Ryan punched a code into the lock on the storage shed, and they slid the kayaks back onto the rack while Brittany shook the sand from her sneakers.

His truck was parked under a streetlight at the far end of the lot, an old Tacoma with a faded surf shop sticker on the bumper.

"I can drive you," he said. "It's on my way."

It probably wasn't, but Brittany didn't argue.

The drive to the rental house took five minutes, windows down, the radio playing something acoustic she didn't recognize. At a red light, his hand found hers on the console. Neither of them said anything.

When he pulled up to the curb, he let go to put the truck in park.

"I had a really good time," she said.

"I'm glad you came." His eyes held hers, and her stomach flipped.

She reached for the door handle, then stopped. Turned back. Leaned across the console and kissed him on the cheek—quick, before she could talk herself out of it.

His surprised smile was the last thing she saw before she climbed out and headed up the walk, her heart pounding, and not from the kayaking.

CHAPTER TWELVE

The house smelled like charcoal and cilantro.

Meredith stood at the kitchen island, dicing tomatoes while Carrie attacked an onion, eyes already watering. At the six-burner range, Lori was shaking a pan of sautéed peppers. Jen was perched on a stool near the counter, stealing chips from the bag that was supposed to be for later. Outside, by the grill, Tom's voice carried through the open sliding door.

"How long on the burgers?"

"You tell me," Meredith called back. "You're the one holding the spatula."

Carrie snorted, wiping her cheek with the back of her hand.

"It's collaborative," Tom said, appearing in the doorway. He wore an apron that said GRILL SERGEANT in faded letters, a Father's Day gift from Sophie years ago. "Marriage is a partnership."

The kitchen had devolved into chaos—too many people, not enough room, everyone getting in everyone else's way. Cutting boards competed for counter space. Carrie's blender concoction sat untouched, bright pink and suspicious. The speaker on the windowsill was playing a nineties playlist that had already caused two arguments, one about whether the Backstreet Boys counted as iconic and another about who had added "MMMBop" without asking.

Ethan reached for the phone to change the song. Sophie blocked him, and for a moment they looked like the kids they'd been fifteen years ago, fighting over the remote in someone's living room while their mothers pretended not to notice. Lori told them to take it outside. They insisted they weren't fighting —in unison, naturally—then glared at each other. Sophie won, snatching the phone while Ethan was distracted. She immediately switched to her own playlist.

Outside, Max had claimed the spatula from Tom and was attempting to flip a burger the way he'd seen done on cooking shows. One smooth motion, a little toss, catch it cleanly on the grill. Lily was stretched out on one of the pool loungers with a book, and Ava was on the lounger beside her, the two of them laughing about something.

The burger cleared the grill grate.

It kept going.

"That's in the pool," Brittany said, leaning against the deck railing.

Max shook his head. "It's not in the pool."

"Max." She pointed. "It's floating."

Everyone turned to look. The burger patty was, in fact, bobbing gently in the shallow end, trailing a thin ribbon of grease across the surface.

Max jogged down the stairs, grabbed the skimmer net, and fished it out. "Got it."

He tossed it in the trash and returned to the grill like nothing had happened. Tom handed him a fresh patty without a word.

Lori finished with the peppers and turned to the blender, examining the pink contents suspiciously. Carrie's creation. Strawberries, rum, lime juice, and whatever else she'd found in the back of the cabinet. She poured herself a small glass and took a cautious sip. Her eyes went wide. She coughed, set the glass down, and pushed it away.

"That's not a drink," she said. "That's a weapon. Carrie, I'm pretty sure this is flammable."

Olivia picked up the glass from the counter, sniffing it. "It smells like a beach vacation and poor decisions."

Carrie brightened. "That's what I was going for."

"About twenty minutes," Tom called from the grill, "assuming Max doesn't lose any more patties."

Max rolled his eyes. "I only lost one."

Meredith pulled out the avocados and started on the guacamole. Carrie leaned over with unsolicited advice about lime juice, and Lori wandered over to watch, still recovering from her first sip of Carrie's concoction. By the time the bowl was done, all three of them had contributed something. Carrie the cilantro, Lori a pinch of salt she insisted was necessary, Meredith everything else.

The afternoon wore on. Ethan drifted outside. Sophie followed not long after. At some point Max handed the spatula back to Tom and joined the others by the pool, where Lily was still reading on her lounger and Ava was photographing everything. Brittany stayed on the deck, texting someone—Ryan, probably—half-hiding a grin.

Tom announced the burgers were ready and carried the platter inside. The teens grabbed plates and loaded up without anything resembling an orderly line, despite Tom's protests.

They ate on the deck, plates balanced on laps and railings, the late-afternoon light slanting across the table. Someone had finally put on a playlist everyone agreed on, or at least one nobody hated enough to change. Lori had added enough juice to her drink that she could actually taste it now.

By the time dinner was cleared and the dishes were done, the sun was starting its slow descent toward the mainland. The teenagers had scattered, and the adults had migrated toward the hot tub. Some already in, some sitting on the edge with their feet in the water, some on the lounge chairs nearby with glasses in hand.

It was crowded. Lori was in the center, Carrie wedged beside her, Olivia on the other side, all of them trying to find positions that didn't involve sitting on someone else. Meredith had claimed a spot on the edge, legs dangling in, watching the scene unfold. Jen had taken one of the lounge chairs, near enough to join the conversation but not quite committed to the water.

Tom appeared and settled into a chair beside them.

"Where are the kids?" Lori asked.

"Lily and Sophie are watching something in the living room. Ethan and Max went for a walk." He stretched his legs out. "Brittany said something about calling someone."

"Ryan," Carrie said. "She's been texting him all day."

"Is that the beach club guy?" Tom asked.

Carrie nodded. "That's the beach club guy."

Tom raised his eyebrows but didn't comment. He was close enough to Meredith that their arms touched.

For a few minutes nobody said anything. Just sat there, the sky darkening overhead.

Jen stood, stretching. "We should get moving. Doors open at eight, show starts at nine. It's about forty minutes to Atlantic City if we hit the lights right."

They started getting ready. Carrie climbing out of the hot tub, Lori following, everyone heading inside to change. Meredith caught Tom's eye.

"Thanks for holding down the fort," Meredith said.

"Go have fun," Tom said with a wink.

* * *

The drive to Atlantic City took exactly forty-two minutes.

Jen drove—her car, her mission, her need to control the route—while the other four negotiated seating. Carrie won the front seat by calling it first. Meredith, Lori, and Olivia piled into the back, dressed up in a way none of them had been since before Sea Isle. Heels instead of sandals. Lipstick that wasn't tinted chapstick. Actual jewelry.

"I forgot I owned earrings," Olivia said, adjusting them in her phone's camera.

Atlantic City rose ahead of them, all glass and light and aggressive optimism, a city built on gambling and the belief that luck was real. The Hard Rock Hotel stood on the Boardwalk, the giant guitar out front visible from blocks away.

They parked in the garage and headed for the entrance, heels clicking on concrete. Music drifted from somewhere inside, not the main stage yet, but something ambient, setting the tone.

The guy at the door checked Jen's name against the list Clint had left, found it, and waved them through.

They pushed through into the venue, and Meredith took a moment to adjust. The space was intimate. Tiered seating facing a compact stage, a bar running along one wall, stage lights already dimmed low. People were still filtering in, finding seats. Not packed yet, but filling.

They found a spot near the front, close enough to see the stage clearly, far enough to have a conversation without shouting. The opening act was just finishing their set, a three-piece rock band that had been decent without being memorable. Polite applause as they packed up.

Onstage, crew members were setting up equipment. Drums, amps, a keyboard off to one side. A four-piece, from the looks of it. Jen said nothing, watching it all come together. She was holding her drink but not drinking it, her eyes on the stage.

The lights dimmed. Jen straightened in her seat, hands tightening around her cup.

The stage went dark for a moment. The room had filled while they weren't paying attention. Packed now, people standing along the back wall. Then the first spotlight hit, and Clint walked out, guitar strapped across his chest, sleeves rolled to the elbows. Whistles and cheers. Behind him, the rest of the band took their positions—bass, drums, keys—and the noise dropped away.

He stepped up to the microphone.

"Thanks for coming out tonight," he said. "We're going to play some songs. Some you might know, some you won't. Bear with us on the new stuff. We're still figuring out if they work."

Laughter from the audience. The drummer counted off. And they started.

Jen leaned forward. Carrie caught her eye, raised an eyebrow.

They played through the first few songs, older material, based on how easily the band moved through them. People sang along to the ones they knew, dancing wherever they could find space. Then Clint stepped back to the mic.

"This next one's new," he said. "Wrote it last week. Still figuring it out."

He started to play.

The melody was slower than the earlier songs, stripped down, almost intimate. His voice dropped lower, rougher. The lyrics were about a woman in a coffee shop, laptop open, coffee going cold. The way she'd stop typing and stare out the window. The way she didn't notice him noticing her.

Carrie squeezed Jen's arm.

Jen stared at her hands, the condensation from her cup cold against her palms.

The song ended. The applause was immediate, enthusiastic. Clint smiled—smaller than before, almost shy—and moved into the next song.

They played for another hour. The dance floor filled. The women migrated closer to the stage, moving together, laughing, not caring how they looked.

The lights came up. The audience headed for the exits while the band broke down their equipment.

Jen's eyes swept the room, casual, unconvincing. "He said he'd find us after the set."

Then her posture changed.

Clint was making his way toward them. A few people stopped him—a handshake here, a quick photo there—but he kept moving, polite but focused. He still had that stage energy around him, but his expression was different now. Softer. More uncertain.

The other four women drifted back a few steps, giving them space.

"You came," Clint said, stopping in front of Jen.

"I did."

"I hoped you would."

"The song," Jen said. "That was me. The woman in the coffee shop."

"Yeah." He rubbed the back of his neck. "I probably should have warned you."

"It was beautiful." She looked down, then back up at him. "I finished the book. The mystery. A few days ago."

"That's great."

"And I've been writing the other thing. The fantasy." She shook her head slightly. "The one that has no business existing. And I can't stop."

Clint stepped closer. "Don't stop."

"I'm terrified."

He held her gaze. "Good. That means you're onto something."

"I should go," Jen said. "My friends—"

"Right. Of course." He pulled out his phone. "Can I get your number? So I can let you know about the next show."

"The next show," she repeated.

"Or coffee. Or whatever." He shrugged. "I just want to be able to reach you."

Jen took the phone and typed in her number. Their fingers brushed when she handed it back.

"I'll text you," he said.

"Okay."

She walked back toward her friends, trying not to smile too widely.

They collected their things and headed for the exit, five women together through the maze of slot machines and late-night gamblers.

Outside, Atlantic City glowed, humming with the energy of people who weren't ready for the night to end. They made their way to the parking garage, arms linked the same as they'd done since college.

"So," Carrie said as they reached the car. "He wrote you a song."

Jen just grinned.

"A really beautiful song," Carrie pressed.

They climbed into the car—Carrie in front, the other three in back—windows down, music up, everyone talking over each other about the song, the show, the way Clint looked at Jen. Atlantic City shrank in the rearview mirror, all those lights getting smaller until they were just a glow on the horizon. Sea Isle was waiting. So was the rest of the summer.

EPILOGUE

The last week of June arrived the way the best weeks do—without anyone keeping track.

The house ran itself now. Sophie worked four nights a week at The Crabby Catch, coming home with stories about difficult customers and the occasional mention of Jake that she thought sounded casual. Brittany had stopped explaining where she was going in the evenings, and nobody asked. Ethan had finally called his father back. He'd stand at the altar, but he wasn't doing the family photos with Tessa or pretending they were all one big happy unit. Kevin had agreed, which surprised them all, Ethan most of all.

Carrie had worked another morning at the farm market. She'd come back with a crate of zucchini and snap peas that hadn't sold, and the names of two women she'd promised to meet for coffee. She hadn't made a new friend in years. Now she had two.

Lori had been to one more event at the vineyard. She'd at last told the others about John—the bookstore, the talks, the kiss by the pond. They'd made her tell the kiss part three times.

Jen had seen Clint once since the concert—a walk on the beach that lasted three hours. She wasn't calling it anything yet.

But she'd caught herself humming one of his songs that morning.

And Olivia was calm.

The change was obvious. Nobody mentioned it. The tension she'd carried since February—the checking of her phone, the way she'd go still when Dan's name came up—it was gone. She'd been hiking with Michael twice more. Once at Belleplain, once at a preserve near Cape May. Everyone knew about Dan by now. They knew about Michael too—she'd told them that night in the living room—but not how often she'd been thinking about him since. For the first time in months, she was looking forward instead of back.

It was late afternoon, the sun dropping toward the bay, when they gathered on the deck. Tom was at the grill again. Meredith had her feet up, a glass of wine in her hand. The teenagers had claimed their usual corners—pool, living room couch, the upstairs hallway where the Wi-Fi was strongest. Sophie was getting ready for her shift.

Carrie noticed it first.

A silver sedan turning onto 59th Street, moving slowly, like the driver was looking for an address. Out-of-state plates.

"Anyone expecting company?" she asked.

No one answered. The sedan slowed as it approached the house.

Then it pulled into the driveway.

Olivia's wine glass stopped halfway to her mouth.

The engine cut. Nothing moved—just the glint of late light off the windshield, the distant sound of waves.

The driver's door opened.

Dan stepped out.

He looked the same as ever—khakis, button-down, not a hair out of place. He scanned the yard, the faces turning toward him.

His eyes found Olivia.

She didn't move. Didn't speak. Her knuckles went white around the stem.

Dan shut the door. Didn't wave. Didn't smile. Just started walking, jaw tight.

Meredith caught Olivia's eye. Lori did the same.

The surf kept its rhythm. The grill hissed. Somewhere inside, a phone buzzed and went ignored.

Dan reached the bottom of the deck stairs and stopped. Looked up.

"Olivia," he said. "We need to talk."

* * *

Pick up book 2 in the Sea Isle City Series, **Sunny Days in Sea Isle,** to follow the group of ladies.

Have you read the Cape May Series? If not, start with book 1, **The Cape May Garden**.

Start book 1 in my new Ocean City series, **A Summer in Ocean City.**

ABOUT THE AUTHOR

Claudia Vance is a writer of Women's Fiction and Clean Romance. She writes feel good reads that take you to places you'd like visit with characters you'd want to get to know.

She lives with her boyfriend and 2 cats in a charming small town in New Jersey, not too far from the beautiful beach town of Cape May. She worked on television shows and film sets for many years. She's an avid gardener and nature lover.